A COWBOY'S RECIPE FOR ROMANCE

Book One of The Billionaire's Venture Romance

AMY PROEBSTEL

Cavaliers Publishing

ISBN-13: 978-1-946292-33-9

ISBN-10: 1-946292-33-8

Printed in the United States of America

Cover art by Wynter Designs

First Printing, 2019

Second Printing, 2021

Website: https://geni.us/LOA-Home

BookBub: https://geni.us/BBFollow

Goodreads: www.goodreads.com/aproebstel

Facebook: https://geni.us/FB-LOA

Twitter: https://geni.us/Amy-T

Instagram: www.instagram.com/amyproebstel

BOOKS IN THE BILLIONAIRE'S VENTURE ROMANCE SERIES

DEDICATION

First of all, this book is dedicated to my friends and family. Your support in helping me carve out time to write and your encouragement to keep me going even when life got in the way, has been utterly amazing. I've been so inspired by your thoughtfulness and I hope it shows in my writing.

Secondly, to the readers of this series, I greatly appreciate all of your kind words, amazing reviews, and support along the way. None of this would be possible without your enthusiasm for the characters and their stories.

CHAPTER 1

Every mile away from the crowds and bustle of Houston made Randy believe it was becoming easier to breathe. After spending so many years away from the ranch, first for school then work, he felt like his heart was finally beating again with the change in the air. Not only could he smell the open fields, he could smell the scent of cattle, horses, and sunshine. When he turned down the dirt road leading to his family's ranch, a slow smile spread across his face as he turned to Katy. "We're almost there."

"Thank goodness, Randolph. Don't these people believe in paving?" Katy gripped the handle over the door of the Range Rover, holding herself stiffly against the rough jostling of the truck.

"I'll have to bring the tractor out to grade this again. It's getting a little rough, but it's home." Randy nodded with satisfaction, looking over to the left for the glimpse of the old homestead he knew would be appearing soon. "The house's just over there."

Katy did not bother moving to get a glimpse. "It can't come soon enough, if you asked me."

"Haven't you ever ventured out of the city, Katy?"

"Not if I can help it," she mumbled, turning her head to look out the window at the desolate landscape which seemed to go on forever. "Don't you have any neighbors? I haven't seen any other houses for miles."

"Thankfully not. Easton Ranch is one of the largest ranches in the world with 825,000 acres, which is an area larger than the state of Rhode Island. We need the room for the 35,000 cattle and over 200 Quarter Horses. Our nearest neighbors are quite far away." Just saying it made him swell with pride. This was his family legacy.

Randy could remember all the long nights spent out on the trail, herding the cattle for calving season and again for auction each year. Those were probably the best times in his life. Nothing could compare to the beauty of this land. It was a part of his soul and nothing brought him more contentment than being back home.

Randy tried to ignore Katy's unenthusiastic attitude toward his family homestead; he thought she would change her tune when she got inside the house. Not only had the entire place been updated over the past five years, it had been added onto significantly until it had become a veritable estate. His father joked about him now being the king of the castle, but it had made his mother happy to keep having new places to decorate. His dad would do anything to make his mother happy.

With the sun just beginning to set as he pulled up near

the front of the house, Randy rounded the circular driveway and parked directly in front of the massive front steps. Shutting off the engine, he turned to Katy and asked, "What do you think now?"

"It's amazing, Randolph! Why didn't you say it was a mansion? Here I thought we'd be staying in a run-down log cabin from the way you spoke of it." She pushed her door open and dropped out of the vehicle, her face radiant in anticipation of staying in such a place.

Katy was nothing if not predictable. Randy knew she liked the finer things in life which he tried always to provide for her. He let himself out of the truck before going to the back to pull out their bags.

Just when he dropped them to the ground, a familiar voice sounded behind him. "I'll take those."

Randy spun around in time to greet their butler. "James, it's good to see you." He pulled the man into a hug and thumped him on the back a couple of times before stepping back and grinning at the old man who had been with his family since before he was born.

"I wouldn't miss the homecoming of the prodigal son," he teased with a wink of his eye. Leaning over, he took both of the bags and turned smartly on his heel to head back inside. Over his shoulder, he tossed back, "Your mother has arranged for your guest to be in the summer room."

Pursing his lips to withhold a grin, Randy merely nodded. Stepping over to Katy's side, he took her hand in his and asked, "Are you ready to meet my parents?"

"Absolutely." Katy grabbed onto his arm with her other hand, practically draping herself over his side in her excitement. Her eyes remained glued to the massive staircase leading up to a deep, wrap-around porch held up by white columns.

Randy had to admit the place looked stunning. With the pride of ownership, he strode up the stairs, already preparing himself for his mother's typical enthusiastic greeting. Even before they made it up to the porch, Randy could hear his mother's squeal of delight that they had finally arrived. He hurried to reach the top before his mother had a chance to launch herself out the door to tackle him.

Just when they got to the middle of the porch, his mother burst through the double doors which James had left open. With her arms wide and a smile plastered on her face, she only had eyes for her son. She jumped up just as she reached him, fully expecting Randy to hug her and twirl her around as he had been doing since he had gotten so tall.

Of course, he could not disappoint his mother, so he let go of Katy's hand and stepped away from her before she could get trampled. His mother felt lighter than he remembered, but her enthusiastic screaming in his ear was more than familiar.

"Let the boy breathe, Lucy," a man spoke from the entrance of the house.

Randy stilled his turn when he faced the front of the house again. Setting his mom down gently, he grinned at his dad and said, "The place looks amazing, Pop."

"Wait till you see how your mom decorated it," he replied, rolling his eyes at his wife's favorite past-time. This was a long-standing joke between the two.

After greeting his father in the same manner as he had with James, Randy finally remembered to introduce his girl-friend to his parents. When he turned to pull her forward, he could already tell she was unhappy with being cast aside for his mother. "This's my girlfriend, Katy Holmes." He turned to Katy and said, "This's Randy and Lucy."

"Otherwise known as Mom and Pop," Randy Sr. put in.

Katy held out her hand to him, which he promptly ignored.

"We don't believe in handshakes here, Katy. Come give me a hug!" He held out his arms, wiggling his fingers for her to come forward.

More than a little uncomfortable, Katy stepped over, barely touching him with her hands as she patted his back awkwardly. As soon as he released her, she was grabbed by Lucy and almost strangled by Lucy's enthusiastic hug. "It's so good of Randy to bring a lady home. We're going to have the best time getting to know one another. Come, come; let me show you to your room."

Katy looked back over her shoulder, her eyes pleading for Randy to come rescue her, as Lucy swiftly pulled her inside the house.

"I see Mom hasn't changed at all," Randy said to his dad.

"Nope, I'm just glad she's got another girl to look after." Pop looked after the retreating girls, shaking his head.

"Another girl?"

"Yes, we brought in another cook. Mabel fell down and broke her hip so we had to hire someone until she got back on her feet."

"I'm sorry to hear about Mabel. Maybe I'll go in and check on her before unpacking."

"I'm sure she'd love that. She was beside herself that she wouldn't be able to fix all your favorite meals while you're here. She always was one to spoil you something fierce."

"Nah, she just liked it when I brought in wildflowers for her."

"Ah, so that's how you managed it." Pop clapped his son on the shoulder approvingly. "How was the drive?"

"Brutal. It's sure nice to be home." He fell into step beside his father. Only then did he notice he stood several inches taller than his father. All those years of looking up to him, thinking he was the biggest man on the ranch, and now he looked down at him.

"It's good to have you here. I just wish we could spend more time with you before we have to leave."

"Leave? Where're you going?" Randy stopped dead in his tracks, hardly believing this was happening.

"We got a phone call earlier today letting us know the yacht is finally ready. We have to go and finish the paperwork and hire the crew to sail it back here."

Feeling as if he had been punched in the gut, he tried to smile and be happy for his parents. This visit had been more than a social call for him; he wanted to propose to Katy and have them all celebrate together. "That's been years in the making. I can't believe it's finally happened today of all days."

"Yeah, your mother's been packing all afternoon. She says she wants to take the first voyage around the Caribbean before bringing it home. I guess we'll be gone for a while."

Randy tried to keep his expression happy, even though his heart broke for the missed opportunity to share an important part of his life with his parents. He would have to come up with another plan for proposing to Katy. "Well, I'm sure we'll have a great evening with you both before you have to go." His smile felt affixed to his face.

Just when he thought he could not take his father's scrutiny any longer, the phone rang, saving him from having to explain himself. Pop rushed over to his office, closing the door as he entered. The wave of dismissal Randy received was nothing new, he knew his dad was a busy man with many business transactions always in the works.

Deciding it was as good of a time as any, Randy made his way through the dining room on his way into the kitchen. Planning on going through the vast space to get to Mabel's private quarters, he stopped just short of the entrance as the most beautiful voice caught his attention.

"Who could be singing?" he murmured to himself. Leaning against the buffet, he closed his eyes and let the melody flow through him. The voice sounded as if it were getting closer, yet it did not register for him to move.

"Oh!" a woman's startled expression broke into Randy's eavesdropping.

Already missing the music, he opened his eyes to behold a beautiful, blonde-haired, blue-eyed woman. His eyes took in her shapely body in one swift assessment before he met her gaze. The lazy smile which crossed his lips seemed to come of its own accord. "Hello."

"Um, hi. I wasn't expecting anyone to be in here just yet. I'll get out of your way." She backed up a pace before she turned to leave.

Shooting a hand out to grab her arm, he stopped her from leaving. "No, don't go just yet. What's your name?"

Gazing down pointedly at where his hand seemed to burn a hole in her shirt, her eyes narrowed as she looked back at his face. "I'm Rebecca Monroe, the new chef. Kindly remove your hand from my arm."

"Oh, I'm sorry. I don't know what came over me. Hey, I'm

Randy Easton." He could have kicked himself for leaving his introduction so late and causing her any distress. "I was just coming back to see Mabel. Is she in her room?"

Instantly contrite for speaking to the son of her employers in such a rude manner, Rebecca nodded, averting her eyes from his face as she looked down at the toes of her shoes.

Again, Randy chastised himself for sounding rude to Rebecca. She had no idea who he was and yet she felt bad for putting him in his place. "I'm sorry for touching you, Rebecca. I just wanted to find out who you were."

"No, I'm sorry. I shouldn't have spoken to you that way. After all, you're a guest in this house."

Raising his hand again, he stopped short of touching her as he said, "Guest or no guest, nobody has the right to touch you unless you asked for it. I hope this kind of thing hasn't happened to you with any of the ranch hands."

"No, no, nothing like that. I...I've got to go check on the roast." Rebecca fled back to the sanctuary of her kitchen, placing a large prepping island between herself and Randy.

Entering the room slowly, he gave her time to catch her breath before he disturbed her peace. Keeping his eyes averted from her side of the room, Randy kept himself moving at a non-threatening pace to the opposite end of the room where he could access the servants' quarters.

He reached Mabel's room and took a calming breath before raising his fist to tap gently on the door. Hearing the familiar voice tell him to come in, he opened the door wide enough to fit his head inside and asked brightly, "Do you want some company?"

"Junior!" Mabel squealed, clapping her hands and smiling

widely. "Come in here and give your Mabel a proper kiss!" Beckoning to him with her outstretched hands, she chuckled all the more as he came into her room and kneeled next to her bed.

"Oh, Mabel, I had no idea you'd hurt yourself or I would've come home sooner."

"Oh, Junior, don't trouble yourself one bit. You're here now." Pressing her fleshy cheek against his, she turned slightly and kissed him on the neck.

She smelled of baby powder and fresh laundry. Memories of her flooded his mind. "You look wonderful, as always," Randy complimented her as he pulled away and seated himself on the edge of her bed. "Is this okay, or should I pull a chair over."

"You better not; I want you where I can hold your hand and assure myself that you're really here. It's been too many years since you came to visit. Tell me all about what's been keeping you away from me."

Randy easily fell into their old pattern of storytelling. He could always count on her for giving him sound advice. After what seemed like hours, but in actually had only been about twenty minutes, he just opened his mouth to tell Mabel about his proposal idea when a knock interrupted them.

CHAPTER 2

Becky could have kicked herself for overreacting to the man touching her arm. After all, it was not like he tried to kiss her or anything. *Where did that come from?* she asked herself, shaking her head in dismay over how her mind had pictured him doing just as she had thought. *I don't have any business thinking of my employers' son in such a manner.*

Her mind went to how good he looked in his snug jeans, tall and muscular, with his confident walk. *Not that I was looking,* she reminded herself. She reached into the oven to pull out the roast. One of her fingers accidentally touched the hot pan, causing her to flinch in pain even as she maintained her hold on the dish. Almost flinging the offending pot onto the counter, she rushed over to the ice-maker and punched the button to dispense the ice. Of course it jammed again.

Almost ready to throw something at the absurdity of it all, she pulled the refrigerator door open to access the ice dispenser manually. After grabbing out a couple of ice cubes, she sighed with relief to have the burning sensation suddenly stop. Once her fingertip had gone completely numb and the melted ice cubes had dripped water into a puddle on the floor, she inspected her finger.

A large blister had already formed. She frowned at it, wishing it could have happened in any other place than the index finger of her right hand. How was she going to practice the new song which kept floating through her head? The guitar strings would only aggravate the problem, especially since she never got used to using a pick. She would have to content herself with recording her voice without musical accompaniment until it healed.

Chastising herself for even thinking about her music while at work, she shook herself back into work mode. Dinner was almost ready to be served and she still had to put the pot roast into a proper serving vessel. Her schooling had drilled it into her about presentation always being a priority.

"People eat with their eyes first," she mumbled, mimicking her instructor's favorite phrase. Since this was only her second full week on the job, she did not dare to cut any corners on her meals. This job was too important considering all of the bills which had mounted up during the months where she had been existing off of her student loans.

She still felt blessed to have come into this job so swiftly after graduating from culinary school. Most of her cohorts were still unemployed. It felt good to be chosen over the more experienced chefs available, although she was not about to take it for granted.

A brief search of the kitchen finally produced the exact container she wanted for this dish. The sheer amount of options available would have made her instructor green with envy.

The Easton family did not seem to cut corners either. Not only did they pay her double what she would have expected upon graduation, she also got free room and board. No longer did she have to keep the lease on the studio apartment in the seedy part of town.

When she was not taking care of the culinary duties, she was free to roam the property. The grounds themselves were a dream. She could wander through the gardens and fields for hours.

The scenery gave her so much scope for her imagination, the songs seemed to flow freely into her mind. Not since she was a little girl had she felt so uninhibited. This place was heaven on Earth.

Almost of their own accord, her hands operated the tongs to place the items on the serving platter in a beautiful, edible work of art. Turning it from one side to the other, she believed even her culinary instructor would have appreciated the mastery of it. With a couple more sprinkles of fresh parsley on top, she declared the meal ready for delivery out to the main table.

Glancing over at the clock, she watched the second hand rise up and brush past the twelve, just as the cuckoo sounded the six o'clock chime. Right on time, she picked up the platter and moved smartly across the kitchen. Using her hip to let herself into the dining room, she just beat the dinner guests into the room.

"That smells wonderful, Becky," Lucy complimented, sniffing the air as she walked through the far side of the room to take her place next to the head of the table.

"Thank you. It's my grandmother's recipe. I hope you like it." Turning the dish just a fraction of an inch more, she smiled at her employer.

"I'm sure we'll love it, if the aroma is any indication of flavor."

Becky dipped her head politely and hurriedly left the room to get the side dishes. By the time she returned, both Mr. Easton and a female guest had arrived in the room. She kept her eyes downcast as she silently finished setting the table.

"I sure hope there's something I can eat here. I'm a vegetarian, you know," the dark-haired woman whined as she seated herself at the table, her expression sour as she scrutinized the dishes presented.

"I'm sorry. Nobody told me you had special dietary needs. Do you like minestrone soup?" Becky asked, attempting to be as accommodating as her schooling had drilled into her and also not let the woman's comments offend her.

"Yes, as long as it's a vegetable base and not a meat stock," she sneered, not even bothering to make eye contact with Becky.

"Absolutely. I'll also bring out some fresh-baked rolls and honey butter." Becky calmly left the room and immediately ran across the kitchen as soon as the door closed behind her. She launched herself over to the refrigerator, thankful she had planned the soup for lunch the next day. There would have been no way to build the proper flavor profiles had she been rushed into preparing it. All she had to do now was heat it up.

Flipping the gas burner onto high, she plunked the pot down and settled the lid to keep in the steam. This would give her a few minutes to prepare the bread and butter before she would need to check on it. Once again, she praised the designer of the kitchen for the ease of use no matter what task she needed to get done.

As promised, she delivered the soup tureen to the table directly in front of the young woman. She smiled as she set the bread next to her as well. "I hope you enjoy it."

"Let me guess; it's your grandmother's recipe." She sneered, looking up at the help with a mean expression in her eyes.

"Nope, it's Mabel's recipe."

"I have no idea who Mabel is, so that's no help at all."

Lucy patted Katy's hand kindly and said, "Mabel's been our cook since before little Randy was born. She's a wizard in the kitchen. I'm sure you'll love her soup."

"I'm sure I will, if you think so highly of it," Katy replied sweetly, smiling winningly at Lucy.

Becky had to keep from curling her lip at their guest's rudeness and fake attitude with Mrs. Lucy. She bobbed her head one last time and said, "Let me know if you need anything else. I'll go retrieve Master Randy from Mabel's room."

"Thanks, Becky," Lucy called after her.

Becky picked up the dinner tray she had prepared for the amazing, old woman and made her way into the servants' quarters. After tapping on the door, she let herself in. "Master Randy, dinner's ready and your family's waiting for you." Using her hip to push the door open wider, she stepped into the room carrying a tray for Mabel. "Your dinner's ready too."

She stepped to the side to allow Randy room to leave as

she seated herself in the chair next to the bed. Holding the tray on her lap until Mabel situated herself, she sighed deeply. "Do you know who that other woman is who's having dinner with the family?"

"Master Randy's girlfriend, Miss Katy Holmes," Mabel smiled.

Feeling as if the wind had been knocked out of her lungs, she could not imagine what Randy could see in such a vile woman as she had witnessed. "Did he tell you that she's a vegetarian?"

"No," Mabel replied as she chuckled. "I'm sure that's going to be a problem here on a beef ranch."

"Only a problem for us in the kitchen. She's quite particular about her diet." She looked up in alarm, not wanting Mabel to get the wrong idea about her. "Not that I'm complaining. She'll stretch my culinary skills to keep her happy as well."

Mabel reached out and patted her hand. "I'm not worried about it one bit. Although, it's a good thing you asked for my minestrone soup recipe earlier today."

"She's already eating it," Becky replied, her voice sounding sullen.

"Everything'll work out perfectly. Trust this old lady. I've seen a few things in my long life."

"You're not old, Mabel. You're in your prime."

"Well, this hip sure makes me feel every second of my life. I can't seem to find a single comfortable position anymore."

"Do you need me to get you more pillows?" Becky's concerns about Katy vanished as she suddenly became concerned for Mabel's comfort.

"No, I'm just complaining. I'm sure I'll feel much better

after I eat that roast you made. It looks delicious. Did you use brown sugar on it?"

"I sure did," Becky smiled, standing up to place the tray over Mabel's lap. "Ring your bell if you need anything. I've got to get started with cleaning the kitchen." She stood up to leave.

"Did I hear you singing a new song earlier?" Mabel held her hands on either side of her tray. She looked up at Becky with an expectant look.

Resuming her seat, Becky nodded. "I was just getting the bread ready for the oven and it just popped into my head. I won't be able to play the music, though, because I hurt my finger. She held up her index finger for Mabel's inspection.

She leaned forward, frowning at the injury. "That looks pretty painful. There're burn bandages in the drawer beneath the phone. I think you'll be able to play your guitar with that on." She nodded as if satisfied with her own answer. "Besides, I want to hear it played. You've got such a special talent with that guitar of yours. You know, Lucy used to sing quite a bit back in the day."

"Really? Why did she stop?" This was something she never would have expected of the mistress of the house.

"She got throat cancer over twenty years ago and the doctors advised her to never sing again. She was lucky she's still able to talk."

"Oh, goodness. Maybe I shouldn't sing around the house. It might make her sad." Biting her bottom lip, she thought back to all the times she just belted out the tunes as they came to her, never once thinking about how it might affect her employer. Her shoulders drooped with sadness; she loved her music too much to give it up entirely.

"No, no, child. Lucy has already told me she loves to hear the music again. She does miss it, but she'd never begrudge your ability to make your own. Never you worry about it again. You just keep singin', ya hear?" Mabel patted Becky's arm, reassuring her with each word she spoke.

"Yes, ma'am," Becky replied, although she still felt a measure of guilt for being inconsiderate. She stood up again, ready to leave. "Thanks for telling me about the bandages. I really do want to get that music set to the guitar. My fingers have been itching to get it done all afternoon."

"That'a girl. I expect to be serenaded in the evening air. Make sure you practice outside my window."

Smiling at the woman's demanding ways, she nodded again before rushing back to her duties in the kitchen. Maybe this evening would turn out fine after all. With the proper bandages, she would get to make her music.

CHAPTER 3

Randy waited until the end of the meal before he brought up his parents' trip to Florida. He leaned forward, his elbows resting on the table as he addressed his mother, "So, Pop told me that your boat is ready to be turned over to you."

"Yes. Can you believe it? The timing's terrible, but I'm so excited to take it out on the ocean and just begin having our private adventures. After we bring the yacht back home, you'll have to join us for the weekends." Lucy beamed with pride as well as excitement of their coming adventures.

"Oh, that'd be so much fun. Wouldn't it, Randolph," Katy exclaimed, her eyes already dancing with ideas of weekends on the water.

"Sure, sounds like fun. Where do you plan to go first?" Randy asked both his parents.

"I don't care, as long as the weather's good and warm. You know how I hate the cold."

"Which is why we ended up getting the yacht rather than a chalet in Vale," Pop teased her.

"You've been just as excited about this as I've been." Lucy playfully glared at her husband.

"Sometimes, I think you only wanted to get a yacht so you'd have something else to decorate."

"Well, I won't deny it was pretty fun going over all of the options with the finishing crew." Lucy patted the corners of her mouth with her cloth napkin. She set it to the side of her plate before turning to Katy and asking, "So, how did you and Randy meet?"

"He didn't tell you?" Katy frowned slightly, turning to Randy and slightly narrowing her eyes.

"What? And take all the fun from you?" He gestured toward his parents and said, "By all means; share our meeting with them."

"Oh, it must be good." Lucy clapped her hands together as if she were a small child waiting for a present.

Katy settled herself in her chair more comfortably as she composed her thoughts. "I was hosting a charity fundraising party for the children's hospital and Randolph was one of the guests on the list. I'd never met him before, but his philanthropy is well-known in the Houston area.

"I had just left the main stage after making the announcement of funds raised so far when I stumbled on the last step. I flew forward, already mortified at the display I was creating, when suddenly Randolph caught me mid-air." She turned her gaze back to Randy, her eyes shining brightly at the memory.

"From the moment he touched me, I knew he was always going to be my knight-in-shining-armor. For the rest of the night, he stayed by my side regaling me with stories of places he's traveled and people he's helped. I couldn't believe how perfectly our lives revolved around each other."

Randy cleared his throat, grinning at his mother's heartfelt look of love. "I was just glad to be in the right place at the right time. We were both surprised at how much we had in common. Even down to both attending Harvard, although we weren't in the same class."

"Even better, you both share the same alma matter," Lucy exclaimed. "You'll never know how many doors that'll open for you both."

"I don't think they'll need to worry on that account, Lucy," Pop corrected. "Randy, how's the business been going?"

"Busy, but it just seems like I've been wasting my time. Since returning home, I can't get the idea of not going back out of my mind."

"What?" Katy cried out, startled at this new revelation. "But you love your job. We have so many friends back in Houston. How could you possibly even consider leaving all of that behind?"

Shrugging, Randy replied, "I didn't say I was going to, but I have thought about what it'd be like to walk away from all the hustle and bustle to enjoy slowing down for a while. You can think of it as a vacation."

"We have too many social commitments back home to even consider staying longer than the weekend." Katy pulled her napkin from her lap, folding it with snapping movements, before placing it on top of her plate.

Randy could tell he had upset her with his talk of staying at the ranch. For the first time, he wondered if she just needed more time to get used to the idea of the slower life. Sudden inspiration struck and he said, "We should take a walk down to the stables and look at the horses. What do you say, Katy?"

"Sure, but I don't think I've packed the right clothes for getting dirty." Folding her fingers primly she rested her hands against the side of the table.

"Oh, I've got just the thing for you to wear. Don't worry about that," Lucy replied brightly.

Randy could see his mother's joy at getting to play dress-up with his girlfriend. He had no idea what his mother would think would be appropriate, but he would bet his inheritance that Katy would not agree with the choice. Unless it had a designer label, Katy flatly refused to let it touch her body.

"Great, we'll meet in the foyer in ten minutes," Pop declared. He stood up and waited for the women to leave before he began to chuckle.

"I bet I know what you're thinking." Randy clapped his father on the shoulder, already grinning in anticipation of what was to come. Having already arrived in jeans and a button-up shirt, Randy did not have to worry about changing.

The men chatted in the foyer for over ten minutes. Upon hearing the first whispers of the women's voices, they turned together to watch them descend the curving staircase. Randy could still recall his mother calling it her *Gone with the Wind* entrance, as they made their graceful way down from the second floor.

Randy did not have to have any intuition to notice the look of fury smoldering under Katy's fake smile. He held out his hand to her when she got to the bottom step. "You look amazing," he whispered into her ear.

"Yeah, only if you think wearing a country tablecloth is attractive. I won't forget this, Randolph." She refused to look at him, instead she focused her attention to the grand front door.

"It makes me hungry for dessert," he teased, leaning forward and nibbling on her neck. Just as he had hoped, she squirmed out of his reach, but she giggled playfully. He had already been forgiven, but he needed to keep her happy.

"How many horses do you have here? I thought Randolph said something like two hundred." Katy turned herself to address Pop.

"Yep, we have 217 of the best Quarter horses around. This last foaling season, we added another 56 foals and fillies to our name."

"Did Princess have twins again?" Randy asked, suddenly more excited than ever to get back into the stables. Princess had been one of his favorite trail horses to ride. Not only did she have a smooth gait, but she was also a wicked racer when she got it into her mind to put some distance between herself and the rest of the pack.

"No, but she had a fine colt. He looks just like she did at that age, all legs with a nice, deep chest on him," Pop answered, warming up to one of his favorite subjects to discuss with his son. Both of them shared a love for the gentle giants, always having special treats in their pockets to share with their favorites.

"Fantastic! I can't wait to see him." Randy kept his fingers entwined with Katy's as he pulled her out of the house. He could feel her reluctance to even step outside, yet his enthusiasm kept her moving. Since the stables were quite far away from the house, they loaded into the work Mule and drove over in relative comfort. Seeing Katy hold onto the metal tubing of the armrest reminded Randy of their drive onto the property.

"Hey, Pop, I was wondering if you'd mind me taking a tractor out to grade the driveway. I noticed it was getting a little bumpy."

"That'd be great, except Walter has it torn down for regular maintenance. Otherwise, we would've had it done before you got here. You know how your mother hates it when it gets too rough to travel comfortably."

"Something we share in common," Katy added, leaning forward so Lucy could hear her.

Lucy nodded, her hand holding the scarf onto her head as she turned to address Katy with a conspiratorial grin, "We may live on the backside of nowhere, but we can at least make it civilized, right?"

"I couldn't agree more."

"You should've seen this place before my mom got her hands on it," Randy said.

"Oh, it was such a bachelor pad. Not much more than a shanty cabin where the boys could put their feet up for the night. No, I'm quite pleased with the touches I've put into the place."

"It's quite beautiful, Lucy," Katy praised. "How big was the place when you got here?"

"I don't know," Lucy frowned, looking over at her husband she asked, "What do you think? About 2000 square feet?"

"That sounds about right. Now it's just over 15000 square feet. I guess we could house a whole army of workers now."

"Not that I'd let them get their dusty boots all over the rugs." Lucy playfully shivered at the idea before she began giggling again. "Do you remember that time when Randy came in from the rainstorm covered in mud? He didn't want to track mud through the house so he rolled all over the entry rug to get cleaned off."

"Yep. I remember having to burn that rug since we couldn't get the mud stains out of it."

"Okay, that's enough of going down memory lane."

"Oh, I don't know, I kind of enjoyed hearing how wicked you were. What else did he get up to?" Katy prompted Lucy to continue.

"Would you look at that? We're at the stables already," Randy exclaimed as he stepped off of the Mule to head inside. Throwing back over his shoulder, he said, "I guess we'll have to wait to have more story time."

"There'll be other times," Katy teased back, swiftly joining him at the entrance to the massive building. She looked around in wonder. "Do you keep all of the horses in this one barn?"

"No, this is just one of four *stables* we have on the property. We try to keep them spaced apart in case there's ever a fire. It would be a terrible loss to the ranch if all of them were lost."

"Oh, that sounds awful. Has that happened before?" She shivered at the idea.

"Not to us, but we've heard about it enough with other ranches. We made sure to plan ahead for it. Right over here; this's always been my favorite spot. Just as he remembered, the smell of leather and cleaning solution surrounded him. He pulled her into the tack room and waited for her response.

She turned around in the large space, taking in all of the saddles, harnesses, and trophies. Walking over to the wall, she asked, "Are all of these awards for your horses?"

"Yep. It's another way to increase our stud fees and increase the prices of the horses we sell. It's been pretty lucrative, not to mention a lot of fun."

"And here I thought you kept the horses only for herding the cattle," she murmured. She turned back to him, a smile growing on her lips as she crossed over to where he stood. Draping her arms around his neck, she leaned into him and said, "I bet you look really sexy riding the horses."

"I don't know about that, but I sure like it. We'll have to get a couple horses saddled so you can see the ranch the way I've always enjoyed viewing it. There's something peaceful about only having the slow movement of the horses and the quiet of the countryside surrounding you."

"Sounds…amazing," she replied, shifting her eyes away from him as she finished her sentence.

He tipped her head back to face him as he asked, "Have you ever ridden a horse?"

"No."

"Are you afraid to try?"

"Maybe a little. They're awfully big and they seem to have a mind of their own."

"I'll be sure to get you a very gentle and reliable mare. You'll learn to love it; I promise." He reached down and took her hand, ready to show her some of his favorite horses nearby.

Once he came to Princess' paddock, he opened the lever and pulled the door open. The beautiful, brown mare lifted her head to investigate her visitor. Instantly recognizing him, she nickered and shook her head as if in greeting. "That'a girl," he called out to her. "I've got someone I want you to meet." He made nonsensical noises in greeting as he crossed the pen, pulling Katy along behind him.

Princess stepped closer until her nose touched his shoulder and the small hairs tickled his neck. Knowing this as their regular greeting, Randy reached up and rubbed her sleek neck while continuing his murmuring. He turned and asked, "What do you think of her?"

"She's beautiful; although, I wouldn't expect any less. Is that her baby over there?" She pointed to the far corner and stepped away from Randy to get a better look.

Princess moved herself swiftly to be in between the stranger and her colt. She lowered her head and stepped toward Katy. With more than a little force, she pushed Katy backward, wanting to make sure the intruder knew she should keep her distance.

More than a little startled, Katy hastily backed up. Her foot landed in something squishy, almost causing her to lose her balance. With her arms pin wheeling, she managed to catch herself with very little grace. When Princess neighed in alarm, Katy had had enough. She turned and raced out of the stable.

Randy rushed to her side, very solicitously asking if she were okay. "Princess didn't mean to scare you; she just wanted to keep her colt safe."

"Well he's definitely going to be safe from me. I'm never getting anywhere near that brute of a beast again. Did you see how she tried to knock me over? She's dangerous, Randolph." She brushed her pants off, only then noticing the smudge of green on the edge of her shoe? Leaning to the side, she asked, "Is that horse crap on my shoe? Do you know how much these cost?"

"Don't worry about it; I'll buy you another pair." By the glare she leveled at him, he knew that was the wrong thing to say. "Why don't we walk back to the house?"

"Fine, but you get to clean these shoes. I may never be able to wear them again after knowing what happened to them."

Randy shook his head in dismay. Waving farewell to his parents, he shepherded Katy out of the barn. This was a side of Katy he had never before witnessed. Obviously, the charity events never involved horse stables, but he never would have thought she could become so irate over a little dirt.

CHAPTER 4

Watching the family leaving in the Mule, Becky felt a small measure of relief knowing she could work on her song while they were away. Now that she knew about Lucy's inability to sing, she felt self-conscious about making any music where she might overhear. Of course, Mabel had assured her it would be more than okay, she still had reservations.

If the song had not been so fresh in her mind, she might have been able to wait until the following day when the Master and his wife would be leaving on their trip, but the song *had* to be played. After assuring herself of the bandage's usefulness, she lightly strummed the strings of her guitar. With her back resting against the porch post, she let her legs rest on the stairs as her fingers picked out the notes she needed.

As soon as the melody came, she was truly lost in the song. This could possibly be the best work she had ever done. Over and over, she strummed the melody while picking out different words to keep the song moving as it needed.

It surprised her how swiftly she had come up with the whole arrangement. She pulled her phone out of her pocket and selected the recording app. Tapping the record button, she set the phone down next to her, and began playing the song from the beginning. By the time she started singing along with it, she was truly in love.

Tears formed on her lower lids, the moisture threatening to drop if she even blinked. She had no idea why this song touched her soul so deeply, possibly because it spoke about how alone she felt. Being around a happily married couple must have stirred something up inside her. She wanted to find that same romance for herself.

Strumming the final notes, she stopped the recording. Only then did she realize she had an audience. A sour chord sounded from her guitar as she jumped. "I'm sorry, I didn't see you two there." Getting ready to jump up and move to another location, she bumped the base of her guitar on the step, making her wince.

"It's okay, Becky; you don't have to go. That was a beautiful song. That was the same one I heard you singing earlier, wasn't it?"

"Yes, I just had to hear it with music." She felt her cheeks growing warm. That last comment should have been kept to herself. Surely, her employers' son and his girlfriend could not care less about why she was playing.

"Randolph, can't we go inside. I can smell the stink of my shoe from here," Katy whined.

"Here, let me take your shoe. I'll get it washed up." Randy ushered Katy to the steps, pushing her to climb up from the dirt pathway. He leaned over and took the shoes from her feet. Holding them to his side out of her sight, he added, "And you can go inside and take a nice, hot bath. How does that sound?"

"It'd be better if you were there to scrub my back," she complained.

"We've been over this before, Katy. There're boundaries we won't be crossing until the time is right." Randy gave her a stern look, like this had been spoken of many times.

Lifting her chin defiantly, she turned sharply and huffed up the stairs, the display made less effective with her bare feet slapping on the steps. "I won't wait around forever, Randolph. Just keep that in mind." She did not bother waiting for a reply before she slammed the door behind her.

Becky turned her wide-eyed stare over to Randy. "Is she always like that?"

Shaking his head, he dropped down onto the bottom step and let the shoes clatter onto the step nearby. "No. I don't know what's gotten into her. Back in the city, she's always so agreeable. It seems like she's been in a sour mood since the moment we turned off the highway onto the driveway."

"I think some people are better suited to the city. Has she ever been outside of the city?" Becky left her guitar lying on the porch as she scooted down the steps to sit beside Randy.

"Not by the looks of things." He shook his head again in dismay. This revelation about Katy's character flaw gave him some real concerns about their future together. She had to love the ranch or things could never work between them.

"How long have the two of you known one another?"

"A few years, but we've only been dating for about eighteen months. She's usually the life of the party. I've always admired her ability to blend with any crowd. But this…this's something too foreign for her."

"Give her time. She might just surprise you."

"Maybe." His reply did not sound convincing. He turned to face her and asked, "So, what's your story? How long have you been a chef?"

Not expecting the conversation to turn onto herself personally, she blushed all over again. She could not look him in the eyes as she folded her hands between her knees. "I just graduated from culinary school about a month ago. I was just as surprised as anyone to be offered this job."

"Well, your meals sure speak for you skills. I think that roast was possibly better than Mabel's."

"Goodness, don't you dare say that around Mabel's hearing. It's her recipe, after all."

Raising his eyebrows, he shook his head and said, "Mabel's roast never tasted like that. You've got more talents than you know." He nodded over to the guitar and asked, "How long've you been playing?"

"Ever since I can remember. My dad used to say my first toy was a guitar. I don't even remember learning to play, it just seemed to always be a part of me."

"Do you play any other instruments?" Randy's interest was piqued. He leaned back onto his elbows where they rested on the steps above him. He stretched out his long legs and crossed his ankles as he found the familiarly comfortable position.

"I can play any stringed instrument as well as the piano. That only came about from needing to hear the melodies which spring up into my head and not having a guitar nearby."

Randy quirked his eyebrow up and asked, "You write your own songs?" Even as he asked, his expression changed to one of wonder. "That was an original song you were just singing, wasn't it?"

"Yes. I just thought of it today."

"Today? I would've bet money that song had already been on the radio. That's amazing you just worked that all out in less than a day. How many songs do you have already?"

"Oh, I have no idea. I have journals full of them as well as some phrases I just loved."

"Seriously, if you had to put a number on how many completed songs, what would it be?"

"Gosh, probably fifty or sixty. They just keep coming to me. I don't ever plan on doing anything with them. They're just for my own sanity, really."

"It'd be a shame to keep that to yourself. You've got serious talent, Becky. You should try recording them and sending them to a record label."

"No way. They're definitely not that good. They're just doodles. Therapy, really. Everything that happens in my life seems to come out in a song. I'm sure my job here at the ranch'll be one before too long. Nobody wants to hear that."

"I still say you're wrong." Randy leaned forward and picked up the shoes from the step. "I guess I better get these cleaned. Although, I'll probably just end up buying her a new pair anyway."

Becky chuckled at Randy's expression. "Save yourself the trouble then. There's a computer in your Pop's office. Go and order another pair."

"Good idea." Randy dropped the shoes and hopped up the stairs to head inside.

Becky sighed as she leaned over to pick up the shoes herself. Turning it over, she noticed the entire sole was red. With a gasp, she realized she was holding a real pair of Louboutin shoes. These probably cost more than she made in two months.

Chuckling, she realized she had just ordered Randy to buy another pair. Of course, he had not even blinked at the idea of spending a small fortune for a pair of shoes. "I guess when you're filthy rich, it would seem like nothing," she murmured to herself as she balanced the shoe on her index finger.

She realized at that moment that her fingertip was throbbing. The bandage must have slipped while she had been playing. Carefully placing the pair of shoes off to the side, she stood up. Taking the stairs, she reached down to gather her phone and guitar so she could head back to the kitchen.

Now that she had recorded the song, she could spend the rest of the evening replaying it. Luckily, she had brought her blank sheet music with her. Before the night was over, she could have it all written out so she could go back to play it at any time. The evening had been quite productive.

As soon as she seated herself at the kitchen desk, her mind refused to focus on the task she had planned. Her thoughts kept returning to the shoes left on the front steps. For some unknown reason, a tune began to accompany the words about the abandoned shoes. It was such a silly idea, she just had to write it down.

Pretty soon, she decided she would retrieve the shoes and clean them up herself. She knew Katy would neither appreciate nor thank her for the kind gesture, but she was doing it more for herself than for the rude guest of the house.

On bare feet, she padded her way through the dining room and outside to the steps. She had just picked them up when she overheard Katy's voice through the window overhead. It had not been her intention to eavesdrop, but the tone of Katy's voice seemed to float through the air so easily.

"You'd never believe how awful it is out here. I mean, one of their horses attacked me in the stable. I was lucky to make it out of there alive. Thank goodness I only have to put up with this for another day. It couldn't go by fast enough to suit me."

Becky looked up, her nose wrinkling at Katy's description of her day's adventures. There was no way one of the horses would have attacked her unless she had done something to provoke it. Which she really could not put past the obnoxious girl. Her thoughts were interrupted when Katy made another astonishing proclamation.

"There's no way I'd even consider moving out here to the backside of the devil's butt. I'm sure I can convince Randolph to sell the place once his parents die and he inherits it. Although, Randolph did say the horses brought in a small fortune every year. Maybe we could hire people to manage it all. In any event, I'll never come back here. You can mark my words on that."

Becky's cheeks began burning with anger at Katy's casual dismissal of the Easton's legacy. She had no appreciation for the art of ranching, she only saw the work of it all. Even as she glared up at the open window, she saw the curtain being pulled away.

Hastily ducking out of sight, she practically held her breath while waiting for something else to be spoken. She bit her bottom lip as her mind raced over what she should do with this new information. Was it her place to warn Randy of his girlfriend's thoughts on the ranch? Would he think she just made it all up?

Hearing Katy saying goodbye to whoever was on the other end of the line convinced her she would not hear anything else. As silently as she had come, she retraced her steps back to the kitchen and then on to the servants' quarters. She took the shoes into the bathroom and kneeled next to the tub.

Dropping the shoes into the bottom, she retrieved the cleaning supplies from under the sink. In no time at all, she had both of the shoes spotless and drying on the rim of the tub. Again, the words of the song about the forgotten shoes came to mind. The final verses came through loud and clear: "These shoes weren't made for a country wife. She just wanted the billionaire's life."

Sitting down on the bathroom floor, she wished Randy would find someone better for him. He did not deserve to be stuck with a woman who did not understand his family's way of life. Unfortunately, it was not her place to say anything to the contrary. If only he could have been her boyfriend, then he would be with someone who loved the ranch just the way it was.

She giggled, the noise echoing all around her, bouncing off of the tiled walls and marble flooring. The idea of Randy picking someone like her over the fancy girlfriend he had was just laughable. He had a type, and it was definitely not her.

CHAPTER 5

"I'm so sorry we had to leave so soon," Lucy repeated as she pulled Randy in for one last hug before they got into their waiting helicopter.

"Don't worry about it. I'm sure we'll be back soon anyway," Randy replied. He glanced back toward where Katy stood speaking with his Pop. If only he could have proposed to her on this trip as he had planned, then they could start planning for their future together.

He saw his Pop pull Katy into a farewell hug. Even from the distance, he could tell Katy still felt uncomfortable with their familiar ways of parting. It was just one more thing he would have to get her used to if she wanted to be a part of their lives.

As soon as Pop came close enough, he pulled Randy into an embrace. "I'm sure your mom has hugged you enough to last a lifetime, but I'll give you one last hug until we see you again."

"I always love it. No such thing as too many hugs. Isn't

that what Mom always says?" He pulled away to grin at his father.

"So she does. I'm really proud of you, son. I don't say it often enough, but I really am. I hope you know that."

"Thanks, Pop. It's good to hear every now and again. I've always done my best, just as you always taught me to do. Like you've always said, 'You didn't have quantity, but you had quality.' That was a lot to live up to, but I think it's made me a better person."

"Yep, I agree. If it had been up to your mom, she would have had a dozen children, but that wasn't in the cards for us. We never felt any lack with you around."

"Yeah, I've heard that plenty as well. I created enough trouble for a dozen kids. I'm sure I'll find out for myself sometime in the near future." He grinned at his father's expression.

"What are you saying? Is Katy…" he stopped, glancing over Randy's shoulder to where Katy stood awkwardly by herself where he had left her.

"No! No, we've been waiting until we're married before we do anything like that. Pop, I've always kept my promise to you about that." Randy could see his father's evident relief in his reassurance. "But, I plan on asking her to marry me soon. I can't imagine anyone being better for me."

"Well then, congratulations, son." He clapped him on the shoulder approvingly. Leaning closer, he whispered, "I promise not to say anything to your mother about it. She'd just talk my ear off about the wedding planning anyway. You know how she loves that kind of thing."

"Absolutely. I'm not sure Katy will appreciate letting

Mom take over everything, though. It's going to be interesting."

"When're you going to ask her?"

"It was going to be this weekend, but now I'll have to come up with something else. It's got to be romantic, you know."

"That's my boy. I look forward to hearing all about it when we get back." With a final clap on his son's arm, he turned and walked away. Catching up with his wife, he reached out to take her hand as they went to the helicopter together.

Randy thought it was sweet how his Pop helped her into the waiting craft. If anyone were more capable, it was his mom. She might not need the assistance, but she loved how gallant her husband could be. Never once did she refuse his help. Randy had a good teacher in his father. He hoped he could be half the man his father was. He had a lot to live up to, yet he was up for the challenge.

Knowing the rotors would begin to kick up dust and small rocks from the tarmac, he hastily retreated over to where Katy remained apart from them. He put his arm around her waist while directing her to move even further away. The last thing he needed was for her to complain about the helicopter wash wrecking her hair or some such nonsense that women could come up with.

Once they were safely back on the front porch, he turned to watch the helicopter rise from its dedicated landing pad. He waved, not even sure if his parents would see him. The pilot must have seen him because the craft shifted and tilted so his parents could easily wave farewell in return.

Seeing his mother's happy expression, he could hardly be

upset with this turn of events. His father had asked him to handle a few items at the ranch before returning to the city. He sighed as the helicopter flew out of sight.

"So, when're we heading back to the city?" Katy asked brightly.

Randy could swear he could hear her planning the trip back already. "Sorry, I can't leave for a couple more days. Pop asked me to take care of a couple of appointments he had coming up this week with some horse buyers. I hope you don't mind."

"Don't mind? Randolph, I've got commitments of my own back home. I can't hang around here in the dust waiting for people to come haggle over horse flesh. You can't expect me to give up my life for this...this." She waved her arm out angrily to encompass the entire ranch.

"I'm sorry, Katy. If I'd known you had other plans, I wouldn't have agreed. I can have the helicopter take you back to the city, if you'd like."

"Alone? Randolph, what kind of weekend getaway is this if we're not even spending it together?" Katy threw her fists up onto her hips as she pursed her lips in disapproval of the turn of events.

"I'm sorry, Katy. I promise I'll make it up to you."

"It's gonna take something really good to make up for this disaster of a weekend."

"Trust me; you'll love what I've got planned." Randy cocked one eyebrow up, a small smile forming on his lips as he thought about what he would do to make her happy again.

"What're you thinking? I don't trust that look on your face. Should I be scared?"

"I guess you'll just have to wait to find out, now won't you?" He left her standing on the steps, her mouth hanging open at being left out of his surprise.

"Randolph! Wait! That's not fair to leave me hanging like that." She raced up the stairs and into the house. Somehow, he managed to disappear before she even made it inside. "Randolph! Where are you?"

He stood inside his father's office, grinning playfully as he hid out of her sight. More than anything, he wanted to get her back to her usual playful self. Several times now, he had seen her acting like a spoiled brat and he needed to know if she was going to snap out of it now that his parents were gone.

"Randolph? Does this mean we can share a bedroom now that your parents are gone?" Katy yelled from the foyer.

Thinking she would attract unwanted attention if she kept this up, he stepped out of the office and tiptoed over to her. Grabbing her arms from behind, he felt her whole body jump as he scared her half to death.

"Randolph, that's not even funny? Where were you? How did you hide so fast?"

"I heard you loud and clear." He turned her around, his face set into a serious expression. "We're not sharing a bedroom. I don't care if my parents are here or not, I'm honoring their wishes and you by refusing. Don't you want our first time together to be special?"

"Of course. Anything with you would be special." She reached up, rubbing her hand along his cheek, down his neck, and finally resting it on his shoulder. "I imagine we could be very good together."

He reached up and removed her hand from him. Lacing

his fingers with hers, he hoped she would not turn surly again. "Me, too. C'mon, let's take a walk. I've got a couple of my favorite spots to show you."

"We're not going back to the barn again, are we?"

"It's called the stables. But no. We're going the other direction this time." He refrained from rolling his eyes at her insistence of calling the structures by the wrong name. It almost felt as if she were trying to be as condescending as possible on purpose. Although, that was not usually like her, so he must just be feeling overly sensitive about everything.

"What time do your parents get to go sailing?"

"Tomorrow afternoon. They won't have their official crew yet, but they'll be able to hire a temporary one to get the first voyage under their belts. Mom said something about going out to Atlantis."

"Didn't that sink?"

Randy chuckled and shook his head. "Not the original Atlantis. Apparently, there's a high-end resort called Atlantis on the island of Nassau, which isn't that far of a sail for the first trip."

"Sounds like fun. When do you think we'll get to go out on the boat?"

"They're bringing the yacht around to a closer port here in Texas. I think it'll be a couple months before Mom'll want to give it up to us. Don't worry, we'll find other things to keep us occupied until then."

"Not anything I want to do," she mumbled.

Randy shook his head at her one-track-mindedness when it came to them sleeping together. He knew she had been with other men, but he had waited. When he first became a teenager, his father had made him promise to wait until he got married. It never seemed to be a problem with other girls, but Katy was different. She had plans for them. Each time she moved him closer to losing his resolve. But now that he was so close to proposing, he was not about to give in to the temptation. He pulled her outside the front door again. Instead of going down the stairs, he directed her to walk along the covered porch until they reached the back of the house. The vast gardens and lawn spread out before them. He took her down the stairs and into the English garden his mother had planted when they first moved out to the house.

"This's amazing, Randolph. How come you didn't show this to me yesterday? I could almost forget we're out in the middle of nowhere while we're out here." She pointed ahead and asked, "Is that a swing?"

"Yep. My first swing. C'mon, let me show you around." He pulled her over to the huge oak tree where the swing was attached to the huge limb. The canopy of leaves made the air temperature at least twenty degrees cooler. He breathed deeply of the familiar scent, directing his memories to all the lazy days playing in the yard with his dog, Duke.

"Sit down; I'll push you," Randy offered. This domestic scene had been something he had thought about doing with Katy almost since the moment he met her. She seated herself as he stepped behind her. With his hands resting on her lower back, he gently pushed her forward.

"What'll you do with this place when your parents decide to retire?" she asked, keeping her head facing away from him.

"We'll move here and run it, of course," he answered without hesitation.

"What if that's not something I want to do? Don't I get a say in it?"

"Of course, but what's not to like out here?"

"Um, how about the fact there aren't any of our friends here? We still need to have a social life. I do, at least. I want to be able to go shopping and throw parties. What about all of my charity events? You can't possibly think everyone'll want to drive for hours and hours just to come out here for a social gathering.

"No, it just doesn't make any sense for our lives. Maybe you could hire someone to take care of it for you. Then you could plan monthly trips out here to oversee it." She nodded her head as though she had come up with the perfect solution.

Randy scowled darkly behind her, he did not like the sound of her plan at all. Maybe he just needed to let her idea marinate for a while. All of his life, he imagined himself raising his kids out here. Never did he dream of living anywhere else. Heck, if it had not been for meeting Katy, then he never would have stayed in the city for as long as he had.

Katy turned, stopping the motion of the swing as her feet struck the ground. "You're awfully quiet. What do you think of my idea?"

He raised one eyebrow, smart enough to know to keep his true opinion to himself for now. "It's certainly something to think about. Luckily, my parents are in great health and have no desire to retire. We won't have to worry about what to do with the ranch for twenty years or more. Maybe you'll learn to love it by then, just like I've loved it all my life."

Katy grinned as if she had won the disagreement.

Standing up, she came over to him and placed her hands around his neck and pulled his face down to hers. She planted a kiss on his lips as if she owned him.

He let her, but something felt wrong. This could not be how his future was supposed to work out. The woman he brought home was supposed to fall in love with the quiet beauty of the ranch and be smitten by the romance of it all. Even the English garden had failed to impress her enough to want to stay.

"We should go back inside. I've got some business calls to make before it gets too close to lunch."

Katy pouted, pulling her arms away from him to cross over her chest. She liked to strike this pose to distract him with her body, only this time, he did not play along. "Fine. I've been wanting to call Bethany anyway. You run along. I'll catch up with you at lunch.

CHAPTER 6

She halted her forward momentum in time before making a complete fool of herself. Just when she was ready to step off the kitchen porch to gather herbs from the garden for lunch, she noticed Randy and Katy coming around the corner of the house. Making a hasty retreat, she managed to duck out of sight before either of them had noticed her.

Deciding she could wash dishes while she waited for them to leave, she tried to convince herself it was not creepy to be staring out the window at them. From where she stood, it appeared as though the two were not seeing things eye-to-eye. Maybe it was the way Katy held herself so stiffly, or maybe it was how Randy tried so hard to please the difficult woman.

Just thinking about breakfast still made her cheeks red in anger. She had kept her cool in front of the family, but inside she seethed at the biting comments Katy had leveled at her regarding the selection of vegetarian foods available for the meal.

Personally, she thought she had gone above and beyond given the fact she had no prior notice to the change in selections. She had to make do with the supplies they had on hand. It was not as if they had a grocery store around the corner to pop in and get fresh supplies.

Randy had seemed uncomfortable about the exchange as well. He had mouthed 'sorry' to her and she knew he meant it. If only he would have told Katy to shut her trap, then maybe she would have felt vindicated.

Still, she stared out the window and watched the couple as they made their way to the swing. Unbidden, a line for a song popped into her head. "The swing won't make her a nicer girl." The idea pleased her so much, she began humming a little tune to the words until the whole chorus arranged itself.

She had been so preoccupied with her internal song-making, she must have missed something about the couple outside. Katy had stopped swinging and moved over to plant a kiss on Randy. Even as she wished she could slap the girl for obviously using Randy in such a way, she could see Randy was not feeling very amorous in return.

With a grin of satisfaction, she began humming the tune again while applying herself more wholeheartedly to the washing. When she looked up again, they had disappeared from her view. Just when she wondered where they might have gone, she heard the front door slam shut and then Katy's obnoxious heels clanging on the steps leading to her room.

Abandoning her washing duties, she turned off the faucet

and wiped her hands on the dish towel. She grabbed up her basket and sauntered over to the door. Just before she made it out the door, she stopped short when she heard Randy clear his throat right behind her.

Jumping, she turned and held her hand over her heart as her pulse quickened. "I didn't even hear you come in here. Maybe we should put a cowbell on you."

Randy threw his head back and laughed. "Do you know how many times I've heard that while I was growing up?"

"Oh, so you've made a habit of scaring people? I'm surprised Mabel allowed you to be such a rascal."

"Trust me; if she could have beaten it out of me, she would have. She gave up early on and started making a game out of scaring me instead. She's really good at it." Randy leaned his shoulder against the doorframe, crossing his arms as he thought back on so many times where he almost peed himself in fright with Mabel's game of revenge.

"Really? I can't imagine Mabel being so devious."

"Oh, she's the best. I wish you could've met her before the accident."

"But then I never would've had the opportunity to come out here at all. She'll be back on her feet in another six weeks."

"Knowing her, she'll be trying before then," Randy muttered.

"Maybe we should be talking about getting the cowbell for her then," Becky teased, chuckling at the idea of Mabel sporting such a contraption.

"I heard that!" Mabel called out from her room.

Randy and Becky burst out laughing. "I should go visit with her a while. Are you getting herbs from the garden?"

"Yes. I won't be long."

"Great. I'll see you in a little while then." Randy sauntered off down the little hallway.

Becky's eyes followed his progress. For some reason, she could not help herself when he was around. Suddenly, he turned and caught her. She fumbled with the door handle and practically fell outside in her rush. His laughter followed her until the door shutting cut it off.

Shaking her head in embarrassment, she hurried off the porch to bury herself in the overgrown rows of herbs. She knew it was silly to think she could hide from him, but it still felt better knowing even if he looked outside, he would not see her where she sat down on the ground.

"What's wrong with me?" she mumbled as she plunked the basket down next to her. Without paying much attention, she began stripping leaves off of the plant in front of her and tossing them into the basket. She should have brought her shears to properly harvest the plants, but there was no way she was going back right now to get them.

Before she knew it, the song she had started earlier began playing back in her head. A few new verses were added and the tune lengthened. Tipping her head back, she stared at the clouds rushing across the sky, chasing away all of her bad memories. The herbs left her mind completely as she laid down on her back to let the song keep coming to her.

Experience had taught her it was easier to let the song finish or else it would catch her at a bad time. Several of her own dinners had unexpectedly turned into blackened Cajun when she ignored her need to create a song. The end of the song eluded her, but she kept watching the clouds swirl, bunch up, and then break apart like they never existed overhead.

A shadow fell over her, causing her to suddenly come back to herself. Hauling herself up into a seated position, she felt the heat rise in her cheeks at literally getting caught lying down on the job. "I'm sorry, I'm almost ready to come back inside."

Dropping down to the ground beside her, Randy said, "There's no rush." He reclined with his hands folded behind his head as he added, "I've been meaning to come out and get advice from the clouds myself. What've you learned so far?"

"Oh, um...I was just composing a new song," she mumbled, suddenly realizing he would recognize who the song was about once she got to the chorus with the swing. His next words caused her to groan in dismay.

"Let's hear it. I promise to be brutally honest if it's awful." He turned his head so he could glance at her from the corner of his eye, a lazy smile forming across his lips.

"I, um, I can't...I mean, it's not finished yet. Maybe once it's done I'll play it for you."

"Please? I don't know much about the song-writing process, but I've heard you sing before and it sounds like I'm hearing an angel. I could use that right now."

"What's wrong? Did you get some bad news from the city? Is that why you came inside early?"

He shot her a strange look at her comment. "No, nothing's wrong really, it's just I'm conflicted about something."

"I'm ready to listen. People tell me I'm really good at listening."

"Okay. How about I make you a deal? I'll tell you what's bothering me after you sing me your new song."

The smile froze on her face as she realized he had caught her well and truly. If she wanted to hear his problems, then she would have to add to them with her song. Deciding to forego the whole thing altogether, she picked up her basket and hauled herself back to her feet. "I've got to get lunch started, unless the two of you don't want to eat at noon. I'm pretty sure the farm hands would run off the ranch if they weren't fed on time."

Randy chuckled even as he stood up beside her. He absently dusted off his jeans. "You've got a point there. How about I help you out? I used to help Mabel. If you don't believe me, then ask her yourself."

"I couldn't ask you to do that. Besides, the things I still have to make are all for Katy. The men are getting smoked beef brisket, corn on the cob, potato salad, and baked beans."

Smacking his lips as she kept listing off his favorite dishes, he said, "My mouth's already watering at the thought. About Katy. I'm really sorry for how she's been treating you. I don't know what's gotten into her. She's usually so polite to everyone. I should've called ahead to warn you about her being a vegetarian. To be honest, I forget about it myself because we usually go out to eat and I can order whatever I want."

Becky liked the way Randy walked beside her back to the house. He was so easy to talk with, even if they were discussing his girlfriend. She wondered if she should say something about the conversation she had overheard the night before, but decided against it. Randy seemed smart enough to figure out if Katy were the right girl for him. She needed to keep her opinions to herself and remember herself as merely being the hired help. She and Randy were not friends; it was not her place to say anything.

Since she could not convince him to let her prepare lunch by herself, she decided to get more information out of him about Katy. "So what kinds of things does she normally order for lunch? Maybe, I can make her happier if I knew more about her."

"Good idea. Hmm. Let me think." Randy leaned his hip against the island while Becky washed the greens she had harvested. The motion of her hands caught his eye. "She always orders a salad. Never with any dressing. She asks for raisins and pineapple on it instead."

"I think we have those in the pantry. Do you want to check? I've got enough greens here to make a proper salad, don't you think?"

"Most definitely!" He grinned as he pushed himself away from the counter and propelled himself toward the pantry.

He disappeared from sight, but the clattering he caused made Becky cringe. It might have been easier to get them herself, but then she would not have the few minutes to compose herself after her ungracious exit from the gardens. There would never be a good time for Randy to hear the song she had composed. Maybe she would play it for Mabel after they left, but she certainly would be keeping it to herself until then.

Holding the two items up, Randy's smile was contagious. "I found them both. The raisins were hidden on the top shelf, but I got them."

"After all that racket, what am I going to find in the pantry?"

"I cleaned it all up," he promised, the cheeky grin returning to his face.

"Sure," she teased back as she plucked the two items from his hands. She pulled out a small measuring cup and the can opener. After saving the pineapple juice, she began dicing the rounds into bite-sized chunks. If only it could be so easy to win Katy over with one meal, but she did not hold out any hope for it. If she were being honest with herself, she really did not care what Katy thought of her, she was just a guest after all. Her biggest hope was to make Master Randy and Miss Lucy happy, they were her priority.

"You look so serious. What're you thinking about?" Randy rested his elbow on the countertop as he leaned forward to speak with Becky.

Feeling ambushed, she jumped and her knife slipped, narrowly missing the tip of her finger. Setting the knife down safely out of the way, she looked up at Randy and said, "I was thinking of your parents."

"Oh? Care to elaborate?" Randy quirked an eyebrow.

"Not really." Becky turned away to rinse her hands in the sink.

"So, about that song you just wrote," Randy began.

"I thought we already finished that conversation."

"No, you said you had to get lunch ready. You didn't say you wouldn't sing it for me."

Furrowing her brows, she shook her head. "No, I believe I told you that the song's not finished. I might decide to sing it for you once the final arrangement is done."

"Hmm. That's not how I recall the conversation going at all."

"I'm sorry you have a faulty memory; that must be rough."

Randy chuckled. "Tell you what. I'll tell you what's been bothering me and then you can decide if you want to share with me after all. No pressure."

With the dish towel held between her hands, Becky turned to face Randy. She scrutinized his expression to see if this were some sort of trick, but she only saw open honesty there. "Fine."

One side of Randy's mouth pulled upward as if he were attempting to keep from smiling. He sighed and looked away from her before drawing in another breath. "I'm worried about my future with Katy. I thought I had everything worked out, but since we got here, she's been different. I've discovered some things about her which were completely unexpected."

"Like what?" Becky could not resist pushing for details.

"Like the way Katy spoke about your food. It wasn't nice and it embarrassed me."

"Yeah, that wasn't very nice, but maybe she was just nervous around your parents." Becky turned away, placing the towel on the counter where she straightened it out for something to keep her hands occupied.

"I can't believe you."

"What?" She glanced over to him, surprised to hear his tone.

"Making excuses for her even after she insulted you."

"I never like to assume the worst about people. You never really know what's going on in someone's life."

"True. Maybe I should sit down with Katy and find out if there's something she wants to talk about."

"Yes, you should do that." She hated the idea of Randy trying to work things out with that viper, but it was the right thing to say. "I think I've got things covered here. Lunch will be ready in ten minutes. I'll ring the bell when it's time."

"All right, I'll get out of your way then. Thanks for listening."

"Any time." Effectively dismissing Randy, Becky began piling the mixed greens into a large serving bowl. She already started planning the side dishes to go with the salad, just so Katy would have the options she seemed to want so badly.

CHAPTER 7

"Randolph, I don't see the point of us having to stay here any longer. Your parents have been gone for two days. I thought we came here to spend time with them. I can't stay here any longer, languishing in the back side of nowhere. I've got commitments back home." Katy stood on the other side of Randy's dad's desk with her arms crossed.

"You want to go back to the city already?" Randy looked up from the paperwork he had been going over, his mind taking a few seconds to catch up to what she had said.

"Already? Randolph, didn't you hear me? We've been here four days. It's time to go home." Katy's tone of finality left little room for arguing.

"Fine."

"Really? We can leave?" Feeling vindicated, a pleased smile instantly changed Katy's dark, brooding mood.

"I'll arrange for the helicopter to take you back."

"Alone? Wait, Randolph that's not what I meant. I want us to leave together."

Sighing, he clasped his hands over the papers on the desk. Sometimes, it felt as if he were speaking with a child when Katy got into these types of moods. In a patronizing tone, he answered, "I already told you I promised my father I'd look after some things while he's away. There's a man coming in from Saudi Arabia to see if he wants to buy a dozen of the yearlings. I can't leave right now, but I can get you back home. Think of it this way, you won't have to endure the eight-hour drive home if you fly instead."

"Well, that is an improvement, but I want us to be together."

"Then stay here with me."

Blowing out an exasperated breath, she shook her head. "I don't want to."

"It appears we're at an impasse, I can't leave and you can't stay." He picked up the phone and dialed the number for their pilot. "Hector, how soon can you have the copter ready?" He nodded as Hector spoke to him. "Sounds good. Plan a flight for one to Houston. We'll see you in an hour. Thanks, Hector." He hung up the phone and looked up at Katy. "You leave in an hour."

"Don't I get any say in this?" Katy scowled at him.

Standing up, Randy walked around the desk to put his arm around Katy's shoulders. "This is all for you, Katy. C'mon, I'll keep you company while you pack."

He steered her out of the room and up the stairs. She felt stiff and angry under his touch, but he could not figure out how to make this any better. "Tell me about your plans for when you get home."

Relaxing marginally, Katy answered, "Bethany asked me to meet with her about planning an event to support local military wives whose husbands have been deployed."

"Sounds amazing. Was that your idea?" Randy seated himself on the bed, belatedly realizing it was probably a bad idea.

As if reading his mind, Katy smiled seductively as she advanced on him. "Maybe we could make this a proper parting." She reached out to caress his cheek, as she came to a stop with her body pressed up against the inside of his knees.

"No, Katy. We don't want to keep Hector waiting. We need to get you packed and ready." He maneuvered himself away from her and stood up. "Where's your suitcase?"

"In the closet."

Randy could hear the barely suppressed anger in her tone which he chose to ignore. He opened the closet and pulled the suitcase off of the shelf. Placing it on the bed, he unzipped it and opened the lid for her to fill it up.

"I'll get your things from the bathroom," he offered, wanting to put some space between them before she could come up with more of her seductive machinations. Walking into the bathroom, he realized he probably should have left the task to her when he saw the plethora of bottles and make-up items strewn across the counter.

"Why did you bring so much stuff with you? We were only going to be here a couple of days," he called out.

Katy appeared at the doorway. "Do you think my beauty comes so easily?"

"Yes. I've seen you without make-up and you're stunning. You don't need all of this."

"Thanks for letting me know I've wasted all my time

making myself perfect for you." Katy had her arms crossed again, her bottom lip pulled in at the corner. "I don't need your help, Randolph. You can wait for me downstairs."

Suppressing a sigh of relief, Randy did not argue. He smiled warmly and pulled Katy in for a quick hug. Kissing her on the cheek, he said, "I'm going to miss you. I wish you'd reconsider staying."

"I...," she began, shaking her head. "Never mind. I'll be done shortly."

Patting her arm in support, he nodded before making a hasty retreat. For some reason, he felt relieved to know she would be heading back to the city. Maybe some time apart was exactly what they needed. If he stayed away, maybe she would realize how much she wanted to be with him. *Don't they always say absence makes the heart grow fonder?* he asked himself.

The devil's advocate inside his head responded by saying, *Absence makes the heart wander.* Even that sudden thought failed to make him miss a step as he headed back to his father's office. He still had a stack of papers to review before he felt prepared enough to meet with the Saudi buyer.

No sooner had he immersed himself in the details of the horses in question for the sale, than Katy interrupted his thoughts by clearing her throat rudely. "I'm all packed. You can send the butler up to get my bags." She sauntered over to the chair opposite him and plunked herself down. Taking advantage of her position, she crossed her legs letting her skirt ride up just a few inches higher.

Randy noted her ploy and did not play into it. Instead, he kept his eyes on hers as he nodded acknowledgement of her statement. "No worries, I'll go get your bags myself. James is getting too old to be lugging such a heavy burden."

"Then why do you keep him around? Honestly, Randolph, it sounds like your family is running a nursing home with all of their aging staff." Katy huffed out a breath in exasperation.

Reining in his tongue, he did not want to bring up the fact that their employees had been with them longer than Katy had been living. They were not just employees, they were also part of their extended family. They were friends whose advice was often sought out and heeded. Not only did the staff hear things from their guests which would never be spoken to their faces, they were loyal to the family. That could not be bought; it had to be earned over many years of trust.

Randy left his father's office without a backward glance. In this moment, he needed to put some space between himself and his girlfriend. To say he was disappointed in her would have been a massive understatement. She had grossly overstepped where it came to who his family employed.

Reaching Katy's room, he gathered her two large suitcases in each hand and turned to leave. As he stood at the top of the stairs, he had to fight an overwhelming urge to hurl her bags down to the foyer without his gentle assistance. Just thinking about it brought a smile to his lips, he could easily see Katy's astonished expression before she exploded with her fiery temper.

He used to be amused by her tantrums, but only when they were directed at someone other than him. Now, he wondered if her nasty habit was something he could continue to excuse or coddle. Either she would have to learn to control it, or she would be searching for a different boyfriend.

By the time he reached the bottom of the stairs, he could see the helicopter had once again landed on the tarmac out front. "Your ride is here, Katy," he called out over his shoulder as he continued out the front door.

"Geez, you could've waited for me, Randolph," Katy complained as she inelegantly clomped down the stairs to catch up with him.

While he used to be amused by her use of his full name, he realized he hated the way her voice seemed to whine while saying it. Pasting a smile on his face for Hector's sake, he set the bags down next to the cargo area and called out, "You made great time, Hector. I trust the weather's going to be good?"

"Absolutely. It should be smooth sailing the entire way, except for the usual thermals over the foothills." Hector exited the cockpit and held out his hand to shake Randy's.

After the men exchanged their polite greeting, Randy pulled him to the side on the premise of inspecting the tail rotor. He knew Katy would not follow, especially with her complete disinterest in anything mechanical. When they walked to the opposite side of the tail, he stopped and said, "I'm sorry to spring this trip on you at the last minute. Katy's insisting on going home and I promised Pop I'd handle the Saudi buyer who's coming tomorrow. Needless to say, Katy probably won't be the nicest of passengers. I'd like to say sorry in advance."

Hector grinned at Randy's explanation before clapping him on the shoulder and replying, "She won't be able to refuse my charm."

"Don't underestimate her," Randy warned.

"Don't underestimate the power of the pilot. If she gets too disagreeable, I'll just pretend to have engine problems. You'd be surprised how swiftly people become grateful when they discover I have their life literally in my hands."

A bark of laughter escaped Randy's lips before he managed to catch himself. "Oh, that's classic, Hector. You're good. Okay, I think you'll do just fine. But if she gets out of line, let me know, okay?"

"Sure thing, boss." Glancing down at his watch, he added, "Rotor up in five minutes, so I guess I've got to get your lady situated so I'll be on time for my flight plan."

Randy nodded sharply, turning to leave Hector to his pre-flight inspection. He continued on his circle of the helicopter until he was back at the passenger door where Katy stood with her arms crossed and the toe of her shoe tapping impatiently.

"Sorry about leaving you so abruptly. We just had to make sure everything was going to be safe for your flight." He pulled her stiffened body toward him, wrapping his arms around her body. As soon as he felt her begin to soften up a bit, he said, "Call me as soon as you get home so I know you're safe." He kissed her swiftly on the cheek before letting her go and stepping back to open the door to the helicopter.

Offering his hand, he assisted her into the seat. Once again, her dress rode up her thighs much farther than he would have considered decent. He wondered if her outfit were an oversight or a careful plan to remind him of what he would be missing. Either way, he was not going to acknowledge it. He patted her hand and smiled at her again. "I'll miss you, Katy, but I'll see you in about a week. I think every-thing'll be squared away by then."

"Geez, I hope so." Katy rolled her eyes.

Not wanting to let her know that her words hurt him, he nodded curtly and stepped aside to shut the door soundly. "All set over here, Hector," he called out.

"Thanks, boss," he said from where he kneeled at the front. "I'll call you once I've landed in Houston."

"Thanks." Randy gave a final wave to Katy before he sauntered back to the front porch to watch them leave. With every step closer to the house, he felt as if his heart lightened from some unseen weight he had not even noticed. He seated himself on the porch swing, belatedly realizing he had not shared the experience with Katy as he had planned so many times.

Sooner than he would have thought possible, the heli-copter powered up and lifted off. He stood up and walked to the porch railing to lean against it until he lost sight of the craft. Just as he turned to go back into the house, he faintly heard Becky singing.

Deciding to investigate, he walked as softly as he could down the length of the porch and around the corner. The closer he got, the easier it was to hear the words to Becky's song. He wondered if this was the song she was composing while she had been in the garden.

When she got to the verse about the red-soled shoes, he had to chuckle. The music abruptly stopped and he realized he had been caught eavesdropping. Rather than duck away, he boldly strode around the corner, his thumbs looped into the tops of his pockets. "It's good to hear you singing again."

Tilting her head to one side, she asked sharply, "How much did you hear?"

"Enough to know it was about Katy. The shoes gave it away." He watched Becky's cheeks turn a lovely shade of pink before he added, "Not that Katy would ever figure it out. I don't think she would actually hear the words of a country song."

"Yeah, I suppose it's not really her thing."

"Definitely not. She's more of a pop culture kind of girl." He leaned against the siding of the house, crossing his ankle and balancing the toe of his boot on the decking. "Can I hear the whole thing now?"

"Nope, I only had a couple spare minutes to practice while I was waiting for the potatoes to finish boiling. My time's up, so I've gotta get back inside." Becky held onto the neck of her guitar like she wanted to strangle someone, and she did not waste any time in leaving Randy alone on the porch.

Randy chuckled again. Something about this girl made him want to know more about her. She seemed to be a contradiction of overly polite and passively aggressive with the words to her songs.

Maybe that was the key; she used her art to vent the feelings she could not otherwise share. With this thought in mind, he decided to pay more attention to the words of her songs. They might just be the key to figuring out more about her.

CHAPTER 8

Becky had to revise her weekly shopping list yet again when she found out Katy had finally decided to go home to the city. Even though it was not very nice, Becky felt herself begin to relax with the knowledge that the difficult woman was no longer lurking around looking for something to complain about. With a satisfying swipe of her pencil, she scratched off the tofu she had planned to purchase.

Walking into Mabel's room, Becky asked, "Do you need anything special while I'm at the market?"

"Can you get me a pile of magazines? I suddenly have a bit too much time on my hands. I may as well get caught up on what's going on in the world while I'm just sitting around."

"Sure thing," Becky answered, grinning at Mabel's positive attitude. Every time she looked at the elderly lady now, she imagined her sneaking up on Randy to scare him. She was glad to know she had a good time all these years on the ranch; it spoke volumes for the family who employed them.

On her way out to her car, she heard a man's whistle sound behind her. Even though the sound was not unusual for the ranch, the persistence of it was strange. Pausing, she turned around to confront whomever was trying to be so obnoxious.

She came face to face with Randy. "What're you doing?"

"Where're you going?" he answered, avoiding her question.

"I've got to get groceries for the week." She put her hand on her hip while her toe began tapping impatiently.

"Want some company?"

Taken aback, she blurted, "Why?"

"Can't a guy just want to hitch a ride with someone?"

"I guess, but I thought you were too busy working on your father's business dealings." Becky looked down, wishing she had kept her mouth shut. Why shouldn't her employer want to go to town with her? For all she knew, he wanted to make sure she kept on task since she was technically on the clock.

"I think I've gotten through all of the papers. Besides, if I don't give my mind a break, I think I'm going to go crazy. Who knew how many different bloodlines could go into a set of horses? I just hope I can keep them all straight tomorrow."

"I'm sure you'll do fine," she responded, turning to continue walking to her car. "I'm parked right over here." She motioned unnecessarily toward the only car parked under the tree.

"Yeah, I sorta gathered that. Do you want to take my

truck? It might be an easier ride over the rougher parts of the driveway."

"Um, sure. I mean, that'd be great."

"Great, I'm parked in the garage." He reached out and grabbed her arm gently to turn her back toward the house.

She glanced down at where his fingers touched her. This was nothing like the first time he had grabbed her, she did not feel threatened in any way. After all, he truly was a gentleman. "Thanks for offering to drive."

"Don't think anything of it. I like driving out here in the country; it makes it easy to clear my mind."

"I totally get it. That's the same way I feel about my music." She snapped her mouth shut. The last thing she needed was to be stuck in the truck with him for several hours while he grilled her about her music. She almost sighed with relief when he kept moving the conversation away from her comment.

"I also like to go riding to clear my head. Do you ride?" He opened the garage door and walked over to the passenger side to open the truck door for her.

"Yes. I love riding. Although, I must admit I've never ridden anything near as nice as the stock you have here at the ranch. I've spent hours watching the trainers and they're something special."

"Then I'll have to take you out when we get back."

"Oh, I can't do that today. This shopping trip'll put me behind schedule for getting dinner ready as it is."

"Then we can go for an evening ride. The cooler temperature will be better for the horses anyway." He shut the door and grinned as she stared out the window at him.

Apparently he did not want to take no for an answer. She

decided to go along with him. After all, she might not get another invitation and she really did love to ride. Turning to face the driver's side, she waited for him to get himself settled before she nodded and replied, "I'll make sure to wear appropriate riding gear. Shall we meet at 8 o'clock then?"

"Perfect," Randy brightly replied, the grin on his face becoming infectious.

Becky grinned in return and rolled her eyes at his boyish charm. She settled back into the plush seat, thinking this was probably the fanciest truck she had ever been inside. It was hard to believe Katy could find so much to complain about with all the beautiful things which Randy seemed to surround himself with.

Randy remained silent until they reached the smoother road of the highway. When he asked his question, Becky wished for the silence again. "Why did you pursue a career in cooking rather than music?"

"It's more practical. I mean, how many people actually make it in the music industry? I needed something which would pay the bills. Besides, my father..." Becky clamped her mouth shut.

"What about your father?" Randy pressed.

"I don't want to talk about him. What about you? Why did you decide to go into business in the city if you love the ranch so much?"

"Touché, although I don't mind talking about my father." He grinned devilishly over at Becky before turning his attention back to the highway.

"Well? Why the city?"

"I wanted an adventure. Plus all my friends from school were trying their hand at business in the city."

"Oh, so you're one of those," Becky accused.

"I'm sorry. One of what?" He gave her another quick glance.

"You don't want to blaze your own trail. You're a follower."

Barking out a laugh, Randy shook his head. "Definitely not a follower. Nothing could be farther from the truth."

"Really? Prove it."

"Okay, how about this. There were six of us guys in college and we did everything together. Before we graduated we made a pact."

"Okay. Whose idea was the pact?" Becky turned to lean her back against the door as she shifted her knee up until it touched the center console. This was not how she imaged the conversation would be going.

"That part doesn't matter," he began.

"Nope. It definitely matters," she interrupted, not wanting to let it go.

"Fine, it was Michael's idea. But let me tell this story, okay?"

"Hey, don't mind me. Tell it how you want. I'm all ears." Becky grinned as she settled in to hear this amazing pact the boys had come up with.

"We agreed that none of us would ever get married."

"What? Have they? Gotten married, I mean." Becky's mind whirled faster than the scenery passing by them on the highway.

"No. But when I met Katy I decided the pact didn't really matter as much to me as she did."

"So you're going to marry her?"

"I planned on it." Randy gripped the steering wheel tighter as he remained silent.

Deciding to let that go for the moment, Becky shifted gears and asked, "Tell me more about this pact. Usually they have some consequence for breaking the agreement."

"That was my addition to the pact. We all agreed that the first one of us married, that person would have to pay each of the other five guys a million dollars."

"What?! That's crazy. That's five million dollars!"

"I know, right! I figured the perfect woman would be worth every penny. Plus, we added another caveat to the pact." He turned and wiggled his eyebrows in his excitement to get her to ask him about it.

"What else could there be?" Becky bit her bottom lip, imagining having five million dollars to burn so casually. These guys really had too much money on their hands to be making agreements such as this.

"The last one to get married would have to pay each of the others back the million dollars."

"So the first and the last get to pay. What about the ones in the middle?"

"Nothing. They just get two million dollars when it's all said and done."

"So you guys just decided to go into business together once you graduated?" Becky continued to shake her head in dismay.

"No, we wanted to, but all of our interests took us in different directions. Reggie ended up in oil and gas production, Michael's in real estate, Richard started an airplane manufacturing business, Markson's a venture capitalist, and Stephen's a Bitcoin Investor. We really couldn't be farther apart business-wise, but we still get together at least once a year."

"So they all don't live in Houston?"

"No. A couple of them still live in Texas, but the others have gone home to be nearer to their families across the country."

"What made you guys get together in the first place?"

"I hate to even admit it, but we earned the nickname of the Billionaire Boys Club by our peers. I mean, a lot of the students came from money, but we all had more than all the others combined. It sounds pretty shallow when I say it out loud, but we felt like the odd ones out and naturally gravitated to each other."

"Yeah, I can imagine how boatloads of money could make you feel so ostracized," Becky murmured, but not quietly enough for Randy to miss it.

"Hey, having money brings a whole other set of problems."

"Like what?"

"Like always having to wonder if people are really your friends because they like you for yourself or just for your money."

"I could see where that'd kinda suck. I never had any money to speak of, so I fell into the other end of the spectrum."

"What does your family do for a living?"

Becky really did not want to go there with Randy. Deciding to end the conversation abruptly, she answered simply, "My mother's dead." She turned her body back to face the front and shifted her gaze outside her side window.

"I'm sorry, Becky. I didn't mean to bring up anything sad

or hurtful."

"It's okay. Tell me more about Katy. You obviously see something in her which isn't apparent to me."

"Is this more research for your songs?"

Becky rolled her eyes and chuckled. "Maybe."

Happy to have made her smile again, he continued, "We met at college. She graduated the year after we did and ended up coming to Houston after we split up to go into our own businesses."

"What do you do, exactly?" Becky's interest resumed now that they had managed to avoid talking about her father.

"I run a meat distribution business. Obviously, we ship the beef from our own ranch all around the world, but I also handle the accounts of almost all of the major ranches in Texas."

"Ah, it all makes sense now. I wondered why the meat was always packaged with the Easton Distribution labels. I thought it was odd for the ranch to package it for its own use."

"Yep, that's my doing. I always make sure Mom and Pop get the best cuts of prime beef for their dinner guests. It's just good business all around."

"Good thinking. Okay, I sidetracked you. We were talking about Katy."

"Yes, she works in event planning for charities with one of her best friends, Bethany. She's had some pretty funny moments in her work, including the night I ran into her for the first time since college. She fell off the stage and into my arms."

"Yeah, I'm sure that wasn't planned at all."

"It wasn't…at least it didn't seem like it at the time."

Randy's brow furrowed as he replayed the scene in his mind.

Becky could practically see the wheels turning in Randy's head as her comment took a prominent place in his thinking. She really needed to get him to know what kind of a girl he had gotten himself involved with before it was too late. If she could guide him there without showing her hand, then all the better. She hated having eavesdropped on Katy's conversation on the phone, but she was glad to actually see her for who she really was.

The rest of the trip was unremarkable as they only talked about little things in their lives. Randy was helpful in the market, steering the cart, and then loading up the groceries when they were through. The ride home turned out to be a much quieter affair since Becky ended up falling asleep as the heat of the day lulled her to relax a bit too much.

The bumpy driveway woke her up. She looked out the window in a daze. "Did I sleep the whole way back?"

"Yep."

"I'm so sorry, Randy. You must think me so rude."

"Not at all, I think you needed the rest. I'm glad I was driving. I'd hate to think what would've happened if I hadn't insisted on driving with you."

"I'm sure I would've been fine. Your truck's just so comfy that I relaxed a bit too much."

"Oh, I see. So now it's my fault for having too nice of a vehicle. Is that what you're saying?"

"You said it, but I won't disagree!" She grinned while she stared out the windshield. The feeling of coming home hit her so strongly, she felt as if her heart skipped a beat with the beauty of the place. She glanced over and saw the same expression mirrored on his face.

CHAPTER 9

Helping Becky prepare the evening meal brought back a lot of good memories of doing the same for Mabel. Randy found his rhythm with peeling the potatoes while he chatted with Becky about the people working for the ranch. He continued to be surprised by her knowledge of how the ranch operated.

"So Jacob is the trail boss. How long has he been doing that?" she asked, her attention only half held by the pot she stirred over the gas stove.

"Oh, gosh. I think he's been here for over fifty years. He came to help my grandfather when he was only twelve or so."

"His parents let him work at that age?"

"He doesn't have any parents. They died of a plague when he was around ten. He showed up here on the ranch half-starved and my grandfather took him in. Little did he know, Jacob would be one of the best wranglers we've ever had."

"It sounds as if most of the people working here have made it their home. How many ranch hands are there?"

"The last I heard, we employ over two hundred hands for all of the various jobs, not just for the cattle, but the horses as well."

"Well, no wonder we get so many food deliveries out here. I'm just thankful that Jacob handles the meals for the ranch hands."

"Yep, he's the best trail boss cook out there. To this day, whenever I smell a camp fire I can taste the smoked ribs he's known for. Have you had them yet?"

"I have and I'd have to agree with your assessment. Maybe you should package them up and sell them at your distribution center."

He could tell she was only joking, but she actually had a good point. They would sell amazingly and he had been searching for another revenue stream to add to his portfolio. "I think I just might do that. Thanks for the suggestion."

Becky turned, her eyes wide as she backpedaled, "I was just kidding, Randy. I'm sure you've got more important things to worry about than my silly idea."

"Not at all, it's a brilliant idea. Maybe I'll call them Becky's Barbecue to give you proper credit." He stopped peeling the potatoes long enough to smile mischievously at her, loving to see her cheeks turn pink at his compliment.

"You better not. Jacob would think I was stealing his idea. You're going to have to name them Jacob's Barbecue."

"No, it doesn't have the right ring to it." He could not resist letting her squirm just a bit longer. Just when she was forming a rebuttal, his cell phone rang on the counter beside the sink. By the time he wiped off his hands and pressed the button to take the call, it had rung several times. The number shown was not one he recognized.

"Randolph Easton," he answered professionally.

"Mr. Easton, this is the Coast Guard."

"Yes, how may I help you?" His heart began hammering as he started to get the idea something must have gone wrong with his parents' new yacht.

"You've been listed as the emergency contact for Randolph and Lucy Easton."

"Yes, they're my parents. What's going on?" He turned to lean against the edge of the sink, fearing his knees might give out. His petrified gaze landed on Becky's concerned expression. She turned off the oven and came to stand beside him, leaning closer to hear the conversation.

"I regret to inform you that the yacht registered to your parents has been unresponsive to our calls."

"Okay, so they must be having an issue with their communications systems. Have you sent out a boat to see how they're faring?" Randy's palm turned slick against the solid surface of the phone. More than anything he wanted to hang up and call his father's phone to get this straightened out immediately.

"Yes, sir. The boat dispatched immediately to the coordinates they radioed in with their mayday. Unfortunately, there's no sign of their craft. Have you heard anything from them today?"

"How long ago did they send in their distress call? Why are you just now calling me?"

"We have protocol to follow, sir. Once we clear the site where we're dispatched to search, then we call the emergency contacts. Usually, we can resolve the situation with the search party, but this time we didn't. I'm sorry to deliver the news of your parents' disappearance."

"So what're you going to do? Surely, you'll keep looking for them."

"Yes, sir. We'll continue widening the search pattern with boats and aircraft for the next week or so. I'm sure we'll locate them, but I wanted to let you know there's a problem."

"Yes, thank you. Can you send me the mayday coordinates? I'd like to organize my own search party as soon as possible."

"Certainly, although you'll need to register your teams with the Coast Guard so we'll know they're working with us and we can track them as well."

"Absolutely. I see your email is listed here as well, is that a good place to send you the coordinates."

"Yes. Can I call you back on the number you're calling from?"

"Yes."

"I'll be in touch." Randy did not bother to say goodbye before he hung up the call. No sooner had he disconnected the call, then he tapped his father's phone number and held the phone to his ear again. Each ring that went unanswered caused him to fear more for their fates. By the time the voicemail picked up the call, he left a hasty message just saying to call home immediately.

"What's going on, Randy? Are your parents okay?"

"That was the Coast Guard. They got a distress call from the yacht but they can't find any trace of anyone on board or the yacht itself. Pop didn't pick up the call, either."

"Oh, Randy! I'm so sorry. Is there anything I can do to help?" Becky gently touched Randy's forearm, letting him know she genuinely cared about making him feel better.

"Not unless you know of anyone who can do search and

rescue." Randy's heart felt like lead in his chest, it almost felt hard to take in a breath. Was it possible to have a panic attack? Is that was he was experiencing.

"As a matter of fact, my cousin and her husband regularly participate in search and rescue." Becky's eyes widened as she began having renewed hope for offering assistance.

"Well, unless he has a boat or a plane and he lives near the Gulf of Mexico, then I don't think they'll be much help." He pulled away, planning to go into his father's office to start searching for private companies to help in the search.

"Actually, they live in Florida and my cousin's husband has his own airplane. It's how he finds lost kids all the time. Please let me help, Randy."

"I'm sorry, Becky. I shouldn't have shut you down so fast. Can you come to the office with me? The guy on the phone said he'd email me the last known coordinates. Maybe you can send them on to your cousin and we can get things started with them for now."

"Great! Just let me turn off the oven and you'll have my complete attention." Becky turned and verified everything in the kitchen was safe before she joined Randy on his way to the office. She wrung her hands on her apron, not able to hide her apprehension for the situation unfolding in front of them.

Randy put his arm over her shoulders and pulled her close to him, thankful to have someone to lean on in this trying time. "We'll find them; I'm sure of it." He hoped he spoke the truth because he had no idea what he'd do without his parents.

"I know you'll move heaven and Earth to find them. I just hope we'll find them quickly."

"Me, too." He left her to sit down in the chair across from him as he rushed around the desk to turn on the computer. In a few seconds, he had his email account pulled up and located the email from the coast guard. "I'll send this message to you. What's your email?"

"EmilyMonroe@asoni.com," she replied swiftly. Pulling her phone out of her apron, she refreshed the screen until the email appeared. "I'll just step out to call my cousin."

"Sure, sure." He already had his attention absorbed in doing a search on the internet for private investigators.

BECKY SCROLLED through her contacts until she found Amanda's information. She hesitated slightly before touching the button; it had been years since she had even spoken with her. If the situation had not been so dire, then maybe she would have tried another avenue for helping.

Not having any other choice, she hit the call button and held the phone to her ear as she listened to the call ringing on the other end. Just when she thought she would have to leave a message, she heard a woman's voice answer.

"Hi, is this Amanda?"

"Yes."

"Hi, Amanda, this's your cousin, Rebecca Monroe." She bit her bottom lip, hoping her cousin would remember her and she would not have to go through the relatives which connected them.

"Oh, sure. It's been years, Becky. What's going on?"

"Well, I actually have a huge favor to ask of you."

"Okay. What is it?"

Fidgeting with the hem of her apron, she sat down on the bottom step in the hallway. "It's my employer, actually, who has an emergency. You see, he just got a call from the Coast Guard saying his parents' yacht has gone missing in the Caribbean. I was hoping you and Riccan could possibly help set up a search party."

"Absolutely, you know we love helping people whenever we can. Do you know where they were last spotted? That would sure help narrow down the area out there."

"Yes, I can send you the email of the coordinates or I could just text them to you, whatever'd be easier."

"Text them to me. I'll contact Riccan and see if he can get off work early so we can head out. Becky, we'll do everything we can to get them back. I'd hate to think another family would go through what my parents did when I went missing for so long."

"I was hoping you'd think that way. I mean...not that, oh, Amanda that sounded so terrible. I'm sorry."

"Don't worry about it, Becky. I knew what you meant. Is this a good number to call you back on?"

"Yes. Oh, and the Coast Guard wants everyone to coordinate through them so more people don't get lost or in the way."

"Got it. We've worked with them on many occasions now so we know the drill. If you can give us a description of the yacht that might help as well."

"Sure, I'll text everything I can think of to you. Thank you so much, Amanda."

"My pleasure. Talk to you soon."

"Okay," Becky said to the phone even though she could tell the call had been disconnected. She rushed back into the office, glad to have good news to share. "Amanda and her husband are going to get started right away. I need to send them all the information on the yacht."

"Jeez, why didn't I think of that?"

"Hey, it's not like we've had to do anything like this before. Luckily, Amanda has and she's the one requesting it."

"What got her started in this, anyway?"

"Oh, I didn't tell you. She was lost at sea for over a year." Becky's eyes grew round as she realized how bad that sounded. She leaned forward, her hands resting on the desk as she added, "Not that I think your parents'll be gone that long. We'll find them soon, I'm sure."

"Look, I don't care how long it takes us to find them, as long as they come back here safe and sound."

"I couldn't agree more," Becky breathed out, practically wilting into the chair across from Randy. "Have you found anyone to help?"

"Yes. I called my buddies from college. They're going to pool their resources and get as many teams together as possible. With any luck, we'll have my parents back home before bed tonight."

"Randy, I don't want you to get your expectations up too high. These things can take time."

"I know, I'm just trying to stay positive. Don't worry." His cell phone rang and he picked it up with alacrity. "Hey, Rich. What'd you find out? Sixteen airplanes? That's amazing. Thanks, man. I'll keep in touch."

Randy held the phone in his hands, his hopeful expression made Becky's heart break for him. She really wanted this to work for him, but something inside her began to twist with angst for the alternative. "Who's Rich?"

"He's my college buddy who owns his own airplane manufacturing. He just let me know they have sixteen of his airplanes heading over there as we speak. They'll coordinate with the Coast Guard and begin searching immediately upon arrival."

"How soon can they get there?"

"Since they're high performance aircraft, it should only be a couple of hours. I really feel good about this, Becky. We're going to get answers faster than anybody else. Since money's not an obstacle, we're going to flood the area with search parties."

CHAPTER 10
(6 WEEKS LATER)

Randy hardly heard a word the attorney said to him. He still had trouble processing the idea that his parents were not coming home again. The Coast Guard had stopped searching after the second week, but his personal search parties had continued for another four weeks. No sign of his parents, the crew, or the yacht had turned up, even though they had widened their search perimeter to five times wider than anyone would have expected.

The attorney stood up, holding a pen out for Randy to sign the document laid flat on the desk. "Just put your name here and here. Yes, that's all I'll need to get the probate started. All of the bank accounts revert to you as well as the stocks and bonds. I'm sorry for the circumstances of my visit, Randy." Mr. Bartlett held out his hand and waited patiently for Randy to shake it.

"Thank you for making the house call," Randy spoke woodenly.

"My pleasure. This ranch has always been one of my favorite places to visit." Mr. Bartlett tapped the stack of papers onto the table top before placing them carefully into his briefcase.

Randy wondered how long he would hear the clicking of the locks on the briefcase as it sealed away his parents' livelihood for the last time. He felt as if he were living through the worst nightmare possible; all he wanted was to wake up and have everything returned to normal. He followed the attorney out of his father's office and watched as he left the house.

He watched the car drive down the long driveway, kicking up small puffs of dust as the tires hit the small potholes he still had not had time to fix. Time lost all meaning as he stood in the doorway. His gaze fell on the horses crossing the far field as he heard them neighing in greeting to one another.

"Come inside, Randy," Becky spoke softly, her hands pulling on his arms to turn him around. "I've got some sweet tea ready for you. Do you want to drink it in the kitchen or the front parlor?"

Knowing he had a friend so close, he turned toward her, his arms wrapping around her. Without even knowing it was happening, he gripped her tightly as something broke inside him. He could not stop the tears which fell from his eyes as he struggled to catch a breath through the wracking sobs which escaped his lips.

"It's going to be okay, Randy. You've got me and Mabel to take care of you. It's okay," Becky comforted him, her hand rubbing in small circles over his back.

"Well isn't this just cozy," Katy jeered from the open front door. "I came as soon as I found out, but I didn't expect to be replaced by the help."

Randy pulled away from Becky as if he had been electrocuted. "It's not what it looks like, I just…" He stopped talking as he abruptly turned and left the two girls staring after him.

"It's good of you to finally show up," Becky spoke. She called after Randy, "I'll bring your tea to the office."

"Make that two; the drive was atrocious as always," Katy called after her. She crossed the foyer and entered the office; her eyes roaming as if she were taking inventory.

"It's all mine now," Randy spoke with a deadpan tone. He dropped down onto his father's oversized leather chair. For the first time since his parents' disappearance, he turned to the canister on the side table. Pouring himself two fingers of the aged Scotch, he did not bother to offer any to Katy.

"I'm here for you, Randolph. What can I do to help?" Katy set her purse down in the chair next to the one she seated herself in.

"Help?" Randy stared at her as if she had spoken something absurd. With a humorless chuckle, he tipped the tumbler up and let the liquor burn its way down his throat. Nothing would stop the hurt inside, but maybe this could make it feel a little less real.

Becky seethed all the way to the kitchen. She wished she could go to her room and scream in her pillow, but that was something she had given up years before. Making a beeline for the refrigerator, she flung the door open in search of the tea.

84

"What's got you in such a tizzy?" Mabel spoke from behind the refrigerator door.

"Not what, who! Guess who showed up on the doorstep unannounced?" Becky held the pitcher in her hand as she used her hip to tap the door closed behind her. She set the container down on the island with a sharp smack before turning to the cupboard to get the tall glasses they used for the tea.

"Let's see. From your reaction, I can only assume it's that worthless girlfriend of Randy's." Mabel's lips turned down into a thin line of disapproval.

"Yes! Can you believe the nerve of her? She couldn't spare two minutes of her *precious* time all the while we were searching for Randy's parents, but as soon as they're officially declared dead, then she has all the time in the world to *comfort* him. Does she really think we'll buy that?"

"It's not us who have to believe her, it's Randy. Given his state of mind, he might just turn to her after all. Don't discount Katy's machinations with him."

"I don't trust that money-grabbing...," she swallowed the rest of her words as she realized Katy had silently come into the kitchen.

"Don't mind me. Go ahead and finish what you were saying." Katy sauntered into the room, for all the world acting as if she already owned the place. "But, you should be careful how you treat me. Once Randolph and I are married, I don't think you'll be needed around here much longer." She stopped at the other side of the island, her fists resting on the marble slab as she leaned forward, eyes glinting dangerously.

"I'm not afraid of you, Katy. Randy'll see right through you once he's thinking straight again." Becky leveled a glare across the island before she picked up the tea pitcher in preparation of pouring.

"I'd like ice in mine."

Becky restrained her urge to grab a handful of ice and shove it in the evil woman's face. Instead, she grabbed the glasses with enough force to shatter them had they been made of anything more delicate. She filled both glasses with ice and poured the tea over it.

"I'll take those. You don't need to check on us. We're going to be quite busy for the foreseeable future." Katy yanked the glasses out of Becky's grasp, spilling some over the edge with the force of her pull. Once she reached the doorway, she glanced back over her shoulder and said, "I plan to help Randolph forget all about his troubles tonight."

Becky watched the tart leave the room. The swooshing of the door as it closed behind her seemed abnormally loud as it made a discordant counterbalance to the heartbeat she could hear in her ears. She turned to Mabel and asked, "Can you *believe* her?"

"Unfortunately, I can. We're going to have to watch out for Randy even if he can't do it for himself."

"But how? If Katy's the one running the show, then how are we supposed to have any influence at all?"

Mabel's eyes sparkled as she turned to look at the door where Katy had left them. "I've got my ways. Just follow my lead. If we're lucky, then we'll have that leech out of the house before the end of the week."

"I wish we could toss her out on her butt right now. I'm sure she's going to insist on vegan options within the next hour. I don't have any supplies for that, nor am I inclined to make anything for *her*."

"I'M GOING to pretend like I didn't walk in on you fraternizing with the help. You're not yourself right now, but I'm going to watch out for you now, Randolph." Katy sauntered into the office. She set the tea down on the top of the papers, careless of what it might be.

Seeing Randolph in such a despondent mood made her realize her timing could not have been more perfect. In fact, if she could keep him drinking, maybe he would be less inhibited. If she could get him to break his vow of abstinence, then he would have to marry her right away.

Leaning against the arm of his chair, she leaned forward invitingly. Her arm draped across the back of the chair allowing her fingers to play with his hair the way he liked. She needed to play her cards carefully if she planned on playing Randolph right into her plans.

"I need space, Katy. Please go sit down over there," he slurred, waving his hand in the general direction of the chairs across from him.

"Randolph, you shouldn't be alone right now. Let me help you through today."

"I'm not alone. Mabel and..."

"You need me, Randolph," she broke into his sentence. Not for one second did she want him to recall that scullery drudge. It had been a mistake to leave him alone with her for so long, but she was going to rectify the situation tonight.

"Who was that driving away from the house when I got here?" she asked, sitting down in the chair across from him. She sipped her tea and waited for Randolph to acknowledge that she spoke at all. She thought he looked pretty wrecked, worse than she had ever seen him before.

She really should have taken the time to come and visit him during the last six weeks. If she were being honest with herself, she just had not wanted to deal with the whole mess of looking for his parents.

When she had heard about the storm which had come up so suddenly in the Caribbean, she knew it was pointless to even look for them. Too many times she had heard about people disappearing from that area. The Bermuda Triangle had more than one mystery surrounding it. Why would this be any different?

"That was Mr. Bartlett," Randy slurred.

"And who is he, exactly?" She looked over to the alcohol decanter and realized the level had dropped significantly. Apparently, Randolph had imbibed much more than she previously thought just on her journey to the kitchen and back.

"My parents' attorney." He swigged another mouthful of the foul liquor, yet his face did not even register the fact he had tasted it.

"So, it's official then? Everything is yours?" Knowing he would not even remember this conversation in the morning worked perfectly toward her plans. She could get all the information she needed and he would be none the wiser.

"Yes. Lock, stock, and barrel. It's all mine, but I'd give it all back in a heartbeat just to have my parents back home again. It's just not worth it." He swirled the last of the amber liquid in his glass before bringing it up to his mouth and polishing it off. "Maybe I'll give it all away to charity," he slurred, his gaze lifting to meet hers.

"You'll do no such thing, Randolph. You're not in any shape to be making any lifestyle changes right now. I suggest you wait at least six months before you make any moves with your parents' fortune."

"I think you're right, Katy. Wiser words were never spoken." He glanced over to the liquor decanter, as if he were trying to decide if it were worth the effort of getting up to get more.

Katy intercepted his plan and placed the second glass of iced tea in front of him. "Why don't you drink some sweet tea? I think you've had enough alcohol for now."

"I don't think I'll ever have enough booze to forget how this feels."

"Randolph, you don't want to forget your parents. Over time, it'll get less painful, but you need to remember the good times you shared with them. It's what they'd want."

"Yes, what they'd want," he parroted back. His hand grasped the slick glass of iced tea. It had sat long enough to create a pool of liquid which had soaked into the papers beneath it. When he picked up the glass, the paper came with it. His eyes seemed to zone in on the words on the page. "What's this?"

"Let me see," Katy reached over the desk and plucked the paper away before Randolph could muster the strength to look for himself. The ink had blurred in several spots, but the intent of the paper was quite clear. "It looks like the highway commission has their eyes on dividing your land. What're you going to do about it?"

"What? Dividing the land? That doesn't even make sense." He held out his hand, his fingers shaking as he waited for Katy to give him back the paper.

She handed it over as her mind whirled with the idea of how this could get Randolph to return to the city. If the property was bought by the State, then he would not want to squander his life away out here in the middle of nowhere. The timing could not be more perfect if she had planned it herself. She would do everything she could to help the commissioner get his way on this.

CHAPTER 11

The first thing Randy noticed was the intolerable aching in his head as he barely opened his eyes to the onslaught of sunlight entering the room. Rolling over onto his side, he stared in confusion as he did not recognize his immediate surroundings. Not only did he not recall going to bed, but he also was not in his usual room.

Hauling himself up into a sitting position, he noticed the silk sheets rubbing against his bare chest. "What the..." he murmured, trying to piece together why he would be half-naked in a room other than his own. Then his mind supplied the answer: Katy.

Her happy singing sounded from the en suite bathroom, which caused Randy to panic. He threw off the rest of the covers before pulling his legs over the side of the bed. Seeing he still wore his underwear caused him some measure of relief, but he needed to get out of the room before Katy reappeared to make this situation even more uncomfortable for him.

He did not bother searching for any clothes; just getting out of the room unscathed would be good enough for him. With a clarity he did not think he should be able to muster after an evening of drinking, he crossed the room. His hand touched the doorknob leading to the hallway when he noticed Katy's singing had stopped. Not waiting to see if she had caught him, he flung the door open and practically flew out of the room.

Looking in both directions, he promptly got his bearings and took off at a sprint to his left. His room was not far away; he would worry about what to do with Katy once he safely locked the door behind him.

"Randolph!"

Hearing Katy's shrill voice calling after him only lent him more speed to his strides. His anger began to rise, knowing Katy had attempted to circumvent his wishes while he had been inebriated. He did not even recall how she had ended up at his house; the whole day before had become such a blur to him.

In that instant, he swore off any more alcohol. It certainly was not going to fix his problems. Besides, he needed to keep his wits about him if Katy's actions were any indication of what she was willing to do to get him into bed.

The relief he felt when he finally reached his room almost overwhelmed him. Letting himself inside his sanctuary, he leaned against the back of the door while locking it at the same time. He fully expected Katy to make an appearance within the next few seconds.

As if on cue, Katy's fist thudded onto the opposite side. "Randolph, what's the meaning of this? You heard me calling after you. We still have things to discuss. Open this door right now!"

"Go away, Katy. I'm going to take a shower. I'll see you downstairs." He imagined the look on her face right now; never before had he told her to go away. She had crossed an unforgivable line. He would not soon forget it.

He felt more thudding reverberate through his body as she continued to pound on the door. Not wanting to listen to any more of her excuses, he pushed away from the vibrating wood to walk over to his bathroom. Maybe a hot shower would help relieve the pounding already happening inside his skull.

As soon as the almost-scalding water poured over his face and head, he felt some tension inside him fading. He opened his mouth and gulped down several mouthfuls of water. With the amount of alcohol he consumed the night before, he imagined he was pretty dehydrated, only compounding his headache.

More than anything, he wished he could sit down in the kitchen with Becky and drink some of her special sweet tea. He missed all of those mornings with her as they planned what they would organize for the search parties. She had been a great friend to him throughout the entire ordeal. Not only had she stood by him, but she also listened to him as he told stories about his family life while growing up.

Resting his forehead against the marble wall, he realized Becky had become more than just a friend over the past six weeks. With Katy's continued absence, he had been able to focus on Becky and Mabel. Both women were more friends and family to him than Katy ever could be. He groaned at how stupid he had been to only just now realize how incredibly wrong for him Katy turned out to be.

Even as he replayed all of the days, weeks, and months with Katy, he noticed the overlying trend. Katy only cared about his family's wealth. She commented on what they could do with all his money; only she had couched it with charitable giving, so he never really considered her own greed.

While he may have been drinking the night before, he still recalled Katy's comments about how rich Randy was now. Even the way she only ever addressed him with his given name sounded pretentious to his ears. Now he had to figure out a way to get Katy out of his house without angering her.

While he had once loved her, he also knew she had a terrible angry streak. On more than one occasion, he had witnessed her schemes to get even with former friends for supposed grievances she had with them. Sometimes, they would make up, but the former friends were now mortal enemies most of the time. He did not want to look over his shoulder if Katy decided to take revenge on him.

Randy groaned as the enormity of his situation fell directly onto his shoulders. Stretching his neck from side to side, he sighed even as he planned to use against her a tactic from Katy's own playbook. He turned off the water and wrapped his waist in one of his plush towels.

Seating himself on the edge of his bed, he picked up the phone on his bedside table. Wishing he could make this call from his cell phone, he had to make do with what he had at hand, considering he had no recollection of where he had left his cell phone. For all he knew, Katy had it clutched in her greedy little hands right now.

He dialed the number by heart and waited through several rings before a woman's voice answered on the other end. "Hi, Shannon. Is Reggie available? This's Randy Easton."

"Let me check. Hold on."

Randy only waited another couple of seconds before the phone clicked several times, and Reggie's voice greeted him. "What's up, Randy?"

"I need your help."

"Sure, anything."

"I was hoping you'd say that. Look, Katy showed up at my house last night, and things got a little out of hand."

"Oh, did she finally crack your shell?"

"This isn't funny, Reggie. My parents' lawyer just left when she showed up, and I already started drinking. To be completely honest, I don't remember much of anything that happened last night. All I know is I woke up in her bed only half-dressed."

"Who knew Katy had it in her!" Reggie chuckled.

"I need to get her out of here and out of my life. It all became abundantly clear last night that she's only after my money. I don't want her to start planning how to make me pay for dumping her, but I need her out of my house. Can you make arrangements with Bethany to have some sort of emergency meeting regarding one of their charities? I'm sure she won't be able to resist taking care of something important like that right now."

"I'm sure Shannon and I can come up with something. Although I thought for sure, you'd be the first one of us to break the marriage pact. I already planned to use that million for a down-payment on a property I have my eye on."

"Ha, ha. Very funny. Anyway, I'm locked in my room with

her pounding on my door. Can you do something right now?"

"Wow, that sounds bad. All right, buddy, I'm on it. Do you need me to send my private jet over to get her?"

"Could you?"

Reggie started laughing even as he replied, "I was just kidding, but since you sound desperate, I'll get them going as soon as we hang up. That way, Katy'll be that much closer to getting out of your hair."

"Thanks, man. I owe you big time."

"Oh, I know. Later."

"Yeah, later." Randy let the phone drop from his hand onto the bedspread. He fell backward and immediately winced at the pain which throbbed through his head. The shower might have helped his hangover, but it certainly had not cured it. He was going to have to get down to the kitchen and eat something soon.

Even as he had the thought, he realized he had agreed to meet Katy downstairs. While he had been joking about Katy's continued pounding on his door, he would not put it past her if she were lurking in the hallway waiting for him. He pulled himself up gingerly, deciding to get dressed and prepare himself for whatever Reggie planned for Katy.

Once dressed, he cautiously opened his door and peered out into the hallway. Unbelievably, Katy was not ready to pounce on him. He kept himself from exhaling in relief, but he still felt as if he was on borrowed time where she was concerned. By the time he made it down the stairs without any sign of her, he decided to avoid her altogether. Instead of turning toward the dining room, he kept going straight out the front door.

Skipping down the stairs of the front porch, he made it to the Mule without being caught. Turning the key to start it, he floored the gas pedal and raced away toward the stables. If there were any place he would be safe from Katy, it was definitely among the horses. She had not set foot near the building since Princess had made her feel unwelcome.

He would have to give Princess an extra treat for her foresight. The closer he came to his goal, the more light-hearted he became. Instead of parking outside in his usual manner, he kept driving right into the breezeway of the immense stable, making sure to stay out of sight of the house before coming to a stop.

Walking over to the tack room, he grabbed a couple of the sugar cubes kept on hand. With a jaunt returning to his step, he went to Princess's stall and quietly let himself inside. The horse snorted in recognition and took a couple of steps closer to him. He held out his offering and smiled as her lips brushed delicately across his palm.

The horse's presence calmed him as he leaned against her shoulder with his arm wrapped around her chest. He felt her warmth as he brushed her soft coat and breathed in her fresh scent. She was able to calm him easier than anything he knew.

A nudge in his side brought him back to reality. Looking down, he saw the little colt looking up at him questioningly. Grinning, he held out his fist for the little fellow to sniff him in greeting. Princess dropped her muzzle down to touch her son's face as he sniffed, almost as if she were telling him that Randy was a good friend.

Time held little meaning while he rested in their company. He wished life could be as simple as it seemed when they were with him. For something to do, he had retrieved the brush from the tack room, and he soothed himself as well as Princess with this even, relaxed strokes.

The sound of a woman's throat clearing caught him by surprise, causing him to twitch the brush into Princess's side. The horse seemed to take exception to the lapse in his ministrations, and she snorted her displeasure. With a sense of dread, Randy turned around slowly to face Katy.

To his surprise, Becky stood at the opening of the stall. She stroked the little colt as she smiled over at him, where he stood with the colt's mother. "I thought I'd let you know Katy got called away for some emergency. You can come out of hiding now."

"How'd you know where to find me?" Randy let his hands drop to his sides, keeping his eyes downcast as he felt embarrassed at getting caught.

"It wasn't hard to put two and two together. What better place to go where Katy would never step foot? C'mon, I'm sure you're hungry." She beckoned for him to come toward her.

Randy nodded, his stomach taking the opportunity of the silence to let out a loud growl. He sheepishly grinned as he heard Becky's chuckle.

"See, your stomach's agreeing with me. You can drop off the brush in the tack room on the way out. I'll ride back with you on the Mule if you don't mind."

"Sure, I'd never make you walk all that way," he replied automatically. Only after it came out of his mouth did he realize she walked out there to go and get him. He felt selfish for having taken the Mule in the first place, yet it had seemed his only option at the time.

"It seemed rather suspicious that she would get called away so suddenly. You wouldn't perhaps know something about it, would you?" Becky crossed her arms as the expression on her face said she already knew what he had done.

"Me?" he asked innocently. Then giving in, he added, "I might have made a call to Reggie before coming out here. How long ago did she leave?"

"The limo picked her up about five minutes ago, but she got the call almost an hour ago to get ready to leave. What made you want to have her leave?" Becky seated herself in the Mule, keeping her gaze forward to allow Randy some privacy.

"She pulled quite the stunt last night. I don't really want to talk about it, but you were right."

"Oh? About what?"

"About Katy only wanting my money. She said something last night when she thought I was too drunk to remember. In fact, I only remembered it when I was in the shower this morning. I can't be with someone like that. I need a partner who thinks that this ranch is heaven the same as I do. Someone more like you."

"Randy, are you hitting on me?"

"What?" His eyes widened as he realized the words had actually come out of his mouth rather than staying safely inside his head. "I'm sorry, Becky. That wasn't fair for me to spring that on you like that. I really do like you, Becky. You've been an amazing friend to me since—"

"I know, Randy. I'm glad you think of me as a friend. Do you want to eat in the kitchen as usual?"

Feeling relieved that Becky had let him off the hook so easily, he nodded as he replied, "I'd really like that. Thanks,

Becky." Once again, she had proven her friendship to him. The tension left his shoulders as he backed the Mule out of the stable and turned back toward his house.

CHAPTER 12

Hearing the news of Katy getting ready to leave
and then actually watching her depart was one of
the best feelings Becky had ever felt. As soon as
the unwanted woman stepped into the limousine, the house
already felt lighter as if the ominous presence were leaving.
She stood at a side window, making sure she was not seen by
anyone outside, just making sure the woman actually left and
did not just pretend to leave.

As soon as the car had gone far enough to no longer be
seen, Becky did a little happy dance at having the place back
to normal. With a grin plastered to her face, she turned to
head back to the kitchen to get lunch started. Already planning ahead, she would get things well on their way before
retrieving Randy from the stables. While she did not know
for certain if that were where he had gone, she had a pretty
good suspicion of it being correct.

"You look mighty pleased," Mabel commented to Becky.

"Yes, the viper has left."

"And we didn't even have anything to do with it." Mabel chuckled.

"What would you have done?"

"Oh, I had a few things going through my mind but nothing was actually planned yet. So, are you going to go get Randy back from the stables?" Mabel kept her eyes downcast to the dough which she was kneading for biscuits.

"How'd you know that's where he was?"

"I've known him all his life. Go on, girl, I've got lunch in hand."

Giggling like a schoolgirl, Becky threw off her apron and called out, "Thanks," as she flew out the back door and down the steps. Her feet kept propelling her forward, hardly even touching the ground as she felt lighter than air in her happiness.

The closer to the stables she got, the more she started to question if Randy had actually planned something to get Katy to leave. She would not put it past him, but she could not be certain until she actually saw him. Her steps slowed as her mind raced along this line of thinking.

Before she knew it, she was standing outside the stables, her eyes easily spotting the abandoned Mule. She noticed the four-wheeler was parked much farther into the stables than what was normal. Another indication that Randy clearly had been attempting to hide his location from Katy. Mentally shaking her head at what he had to go through made her wish she could erase all of the heartache he had been going through lately.

Nodding to herself that she had been correct in her guess of his location, she entered the shaded, cool interior. Immediately, her sense of smell was assaulted with the smell of leather, hay, and horses. She breathed in deeply, her mind whirling back to all her childhood horse riding lessons she had taken.

She let the murmuring of a man's voice lead her to the stall where she saw Randy with his favorite horse. Just seeing him pour his love into every brush stroke made her heart skip a beat. This gentle man deserved so much better than Katy could ever give him. She hoped he would come to the same conclusion before he made the mistake of asking her to marry him.

Not that it's any of my business, she thought to herself. *After all, I'm only the hired help*. She cleared her throat, bringing herself back to the task she had at present. When he looked over at her, an almost comical combination of fear and relief crossed over his features.

Deciding to let him off the hook promptly, she said, "I thought I'd let you know Katy got called away for some emergency. You can come out of hiding now."

"How'd you know where to find me?"

"It wasn't hard to put two and two together. What better place to go where Katy would never step foot? C'mon; I'm sure you're hungry." Watching the tension immediately leave Randy's posture, she knew her initial assessment of him having something to do with her abrupt departure was correct. "It seemed rather suspicious that she would get called away so suddenly. You wouldn't perhaps know something about it, would you?"

"Me?" he asked, entirely too innocent to be believable.

Hearing him admit to his part in the scheme to get Katy called away gave her hope for Randy seeing through the woman's scheming. Seeing this playful side of Randy also let her know that he was recovering from the shock of his parents' sudden demise. Thinking of her own mother's passing still broke her heart, she could only imagine how losing both parents at the same time would be quite devastating.

Hearing his stomach growl at the mention of food only confirmed her suspicions further. "See; your stomach's agreeing with me. You can drop off the brush in the tack room on the way out. I'll ride back with you on the Mule, if you don't mind."

"Sure, I'd never make you walk all that way."

Following him to the tack room, she noted how he had lost weight in the last six weeks, even with her best efforts to entice him to eat food. Maybe now that everything had been resolved once and for all, he could begin the mending process.

Hearing him tell her about what Katy had disclosed the night before made Becky's blood boil. It was bad enough for the woman to show up unannounced, but to boldly declare her desire to have all his money was low even for Katy. Thankfully, Randy seemed ready to distance himself from her for the time being; hopefully, he would make it permanent.

When Randy got to the part of his story about wishing for someone like herself, Becky could have jumped for joy. "Randy, are you hitting on me?" she teased, grinning to keep the conversation light, but her stomach began to flutter with the unexpected compliment. Maybe she had a chance with him after all. Why else would he say something like that?

"What?"

Randy's cheeks reddened slightly but Becky noticed he did not deny her accusation.

"I'm sorry, Becky. That wasn't fair for me to spring that on you like that. I really do like you, Becky. You've been an amazing friend to me since..."

"I know, Randy. I'm glad you think of me as a friend." *I think I actually have a chance of it becoming something more than that,* she thought to herself. Keeping her voice calm, she asked, "Do you want to eat in the kitchen as usual?"

"I'd really like that. Thanks, Becky."

Deciding to let the conversation go for now, Becky kept her gaze anywhere but in Randy's direction. The beautiful landscape surrounding them gave her such an inner peace, she wondered if Randy appreciated it on the same level as she always did. Something inside her told her he must since all of his stories about his childhood were so colorfully told with reminiscing over the changing seasons of the land around him.

Rather than parking in front of the house, Randy pulled the Mule around to the back door. After parking, he waited on his side for Becky to catch up with him. She promptly jumped out of the vehicle and rounded the back of it to walk up the stairs with him. He seemed rather eager to eat. "How's your head this morning?"

"Ugh, don't ask. I should've had a lot more water last night or this morning, but..."

"I know; you had to hide out for a while. I'll make sure you get plenty to drink with breakfast." She glanced at her watch before amending, "Lunch, actually."

"I feel like it's been a month since my last meal." He held

open the door for Becky before following her inside. "Where's Mabel?"

"I don't know," she answered, spying the two plates laid out on the island. She narrowed her eyes at what the old cook was up to. "I'll go check on her. Go ahead and get started."

Becky veered off to the right into the servants' quarters, barely pausing after knocking on Mabel's door. Hearing the woman inside telling her to enter, Becky opened the door and peered inside. "What's going on?" She could see a plate of food on the tray over Mabel's lap.

"My hip started hurting so I thought I'd take a little rest while eating lunch. Go ahead and enjoy your time with Randy." The glint in Mabel's eyes spoke more than her words.

Knowing Mabel had planned all of this was not lost on Becky, but she did not object to it either. After all, Mabel had known Randy all his life and she wanted him to be happy. On more than one occasion, Mabel had said how good Becky would be for him, this must just be her way of setting things up for the two of them. "Thanks. I'll let Randy know you're okay."

"And I think I might take a nap after I finish eating. I'll be out to help you with dinner."

"Okay. Have a good nap, then," Becky let herself out of the room, not missing the woman's pleased expression. She returned to the kitchen and seated herself next to Randy. Picking up her fork, she said, "Mabel's resting her hip, but she says she's doing just fine." After eating a bite of the biscuits and gravy, she added, "I believe she's trying to give the two of us time alone together."

"I was just thinking the exact same thing. I'm not bothered by it. Are you?" He put his fork down before turning his body toward her to wait for her answer.

Becky appraised his posture as well as the earnest expression on his face. She shook her head, and answered, "Not at all."

Nodding his acknowledgment of her answer, he resumed eating. She watched him carefully, noting his ease had become somewhat stilted. Trying to act casual about the whole thing, she asked, "Do you think you'll get back together with Katy?"

"No!" he almost yelled in his haste.

Becky raised her eyebrows at his vehement protest.

"I mean, I can't be with her. She's not the woman I thought she was and she never will be. These last six weeks only pointed out how selfish she can be. I needed her the most and yet she was too busy to even pick up the phone to ask how I was doing."

"What if she had a good excuse?"

"What excuse could that be?"

"I don't know. I just thought she would probably come up with something to get you to forgive her."

"Nope. That's not going to happen. I'm officially single again." He glanced over to Becky and asked, "Do you think that makes me shallow? I mean, what if I wanted to move on?"

"No, I don't think you're shallow at all. But I do think you should take the time to heal before you dive into another relationship."

"Even if I wanted one with you?"

"Well, that might be different. Now that you put it that way."

Randy smiled and put another bite of biscuit into his mouth, his eyes never leaving hers. The silence continued, broken only by the clinking of the silverware on the plates. Neither of them wanted to say something wrong, but something needed to be said.

"I guess I was right earlier when I accused you of hitting on me, then," Becky mused, her eyes focused on her plate. It was nerve-wracking to put herself out there with Randy. If she were wrong, then it might cost her her job.

"Yes. I was just too blind to see how perfect you are for me."

"Well, everyone has flaws."

Randy laughed, a genuine sound coming straight from his gut. Becky loved hearing the sound. "I guess that means you're not going to fire me."

Another laugh followed her statement, causing Becky to grin even wider. While she still did not know where this relationship would go, she hoped she could at least help him heal from his failed one with Katy. On a more serious note she added, "Although I do worry about how fast you're moving on. I mean, does that make me a rebound relationship?"

"Maybe, but who's to say that it won't work out perfectly. I mean, we've already got Mabel working on setting us up. She would never steer me wrong."

"Yes, I keep hearing about how she's known you all of your life."

"Yes. She's like a second mom to me." Even as the words

came out of his mouth, he began to choke up. "She's my only mom now."

Becky dropped her fork and scooted off her chair in order to stand beside Randy. To her surprise, he turned to her and put his arms around her as he burst into tears. This was the first time he had actually let go enough to let his feelings pour out. This was the turning point she had been watching for, yet it did not make it any easier to witness.

"Let it out, Randy, let it all out. It's going to hurt for a long time, but each day will get easier. I'm so sorry you're hurting so much." Becky continued to repeat the same words over and over as she rubbed his back and held him tight to her. Her heart broke for him, but she knew he needed this release before he would start to heal.

CHAPTER 13

Feeling ashamed at breaking down so thoroughly in front of Becky during lunch, Randy made himself scarce for the remainder of the afternoon. He shut himself away in his father's office and studied the paperwork left on the desk. His attention was caught by the watermarks of a glass on a certain paper.

Picking it up, he leaned toward the light of the window to be able to read the blurred writing. As soon as the meaning of the notice finally got through to his brain, he stood up and began pacing with angry strides. "How's this even possible," he cried out to himself. "I don't have the energy to fight with the State over land rights."

Realizing he did not have to do it alone, he rushed to sit back down at the desk and thumb through his father's Rolodex until he got to Mr. Bartlett's listing. He dialed the number and waited through several rings before the answering machine kicked on. Looking over at the clock, he realized it was after business hours so he left a brief message asking him to return his call as soon as he could in the morning.

After hanging up the phone, he inhaled sharply as he tried to control the anger rising up inside him. Surely his father knew about this matter. The letter clearly talked about this being referenced before, yet his father had said nothing to him. Hopefully a plan was already in place and he just needed to be let into the loop on the matter.

The walls seemed to be closing in on him; he had to get out of the office. Maybe some time out on the porch would do him some good. Liking the idea more than anything else at the moment, he left the house and paced on the porch instead. Not more than two minutes had passed before he realized he could hear Becky singing around back.

Walking along the edge of the house, he walked quietly so as not to disturb her singing. Hearing her voice carrying on the soft breeze soothed his frayed nerves and he wanted her to continue. Just as he got to the area he suspected she would be, his foot caught on the edge of the rocking chair and caused a loud crack of the wood backing to hit the side of the house.

Becky whirled around, her mouth rounded into a surprised expression and her fingers stilled on the strings of her guitar. "Oh, I didn't hear you coming. I'll go get dinner served."

"No, please don't. I'd appreciate it if you'd keep singing." He seated himself in the rocking chair he had grabbed to still it from thumping more. A cat strolled away from Becky's side to rub against his pant legs. He leaned forward and stroked the silky fur along the tom cat's back. "Is this one yours?"

"No, but he acts like he's supposed to be." She laughed as she remembered something. "The other day, he followed me into the house and about scared me to death by rubbing against the back of my legs while I was tending a pot on the stove. I had no idea he had ghosted himself inside. He's quite the fiend."

Randy smiled down at the cat who had stopped to look up at him with his bright green eyes. "Are you a rascal?" The cat let out a small meow as if answering. Both Randy and Becky broke out laughing at the perfect timing of the cat's response.

"Maybe he should be named Rascal."

"Sounds good." He looked over at Becky and saw the loving expression on her face as she watched the cat. "You know I don't mind if he comes in the house. We always had house cats when I was growing up."

"Really? I'd like that a lot. I miss having a pet."

"Absolutely." Randy stood up and walked over to sit next to Becky on the step, hoping the cat would follow him. Just as planned, the cat strolled over and let himself up onto Randy's lap. He imagined the cat would have preferred Becky's lap, except it was already filled with her guitar. "What're you playing? It sounded really nice before I scared you."

"Oh, it's an old song I wrote when I was a kid. I tend to sing it when I'm really happy."

"Are you then? Happy, I mean."

"Yes. I am. You make me happy, Randy."

"I'm glad. You make me happy, too." He glanced over to her, enjoying the way the soft light of the setting sun glinted in her eyes. She was absolutely beautiful. How come he had not noticed that before? Could it be he was so focused on being with Katy that he had failed to see her radiance? His breath caught in his throat as he continued to stare at her.

"Are you okay?"

Her question took a second to register. Shaking his head, he blinked several times and blurted, "You're beautiful."

She looked away, the edge of her mouth turning up as she tried to resist a smile. Her cheek blushed even more as she stammered, "Um, thanks."

"I'm sorry. I didn't mean to blurt that out like that. But it is true." He looked down at Rascal to pet the cat which was now curled up in a furry ball on his lap. He really knew how to stick his foot in his mouth.

Becky's fingers strummed a few notes on her guitar before she started singing softly again. Apparently, she felt more comfortable singing beside him than hearing him talk. At this point, he would agree with her assessment of the situation. He closed his eyes and let her music flow through him.

Her tone was so pure, her playing so simple yet effective in emphasizing the words of her song. It was a brilliant performance. When he opened his eyes at the end of the song, he smiled and said, "That was amazing. You should record that."

"Oh, no. I don't have any way to get that done right. I mean, I record almost everything I create on my phone, but that's only so I can make sure to remember it as it comes to me. As soon as I'm able, I transcribe it onto sheet music."

"Wow, you can read music as well? Your skills never cease to amaze me." Randy looked out over the darkening landscape, watching the shadows grow against the back lawn. This was one of his favorite times of the day with the crickets beginning their evening song and the cooler night breezes brushing against him. Having Becky beside him made it all the more perfect.

This was what he had imagined for himself with Katy. *Where had that thought come from?* He wondered. "Do you want to go for an evening ride with me?"

"Really? I'd love to go riding."

"Great, then it's settled. I'll have the groom saddle up two horses for us and we can ride the countryside by moonlight." He glanced up at the almost perfect circle of the moon's face already brightening the sky.

Gently repositioning the cat onto the deck, Randy pushed himself up from the step and grinned while looking down at Becky. "I'll go make the arrangements and meet you out front in five minutes. Does that work for you?"

"Eee, I'm going to have to hurry. I still have to change into appropriate riding clothes and put my guitar away." She took the hand he offered her and stood beside him. "Yes, I'll have just enough time."

"Great. See you in a few." Randy lengthened his stride as he walked over to the door to hold it open for Becky. He followed her into the kitchen and continued on until he got to his office. *My father's office*, he reminded himself. His mood dampened slightly as he unconsciously started to erase his parents from the house.

Once inside, he picked up the direct line to the stables and requested the horses be made ready. The grooms were such professionals that they did not ask any questions about the late hour, only the skill of the second rider. "I think she can handle Donas. It's for Becky."

"Will do. They'll be ready by the time you get here."

"Thanks, Johnny."

He leaned against the edge of the desk, looking down at his own attire. Thinking his jeans would be fine for riding, he decided not to change. Instead, he would rather wait for Becky out on the front porch.

Seated on the porch swing, he felt as though he had been propelled back in time to his childhood. So many evenings had been spent out there, rocking slightly and waiting for any shooting stars to happen over the horizon.

"I'm ready," Becky spoke beside him.

"Oh, I didn't hear you. If I didn't know better, I'd think you've been getting lessons from Mabel." He stood up and held out his hand for Becky. "I don't want you to stumble down the steps," he assured her, yet really he just wanted to feel the warmth of her skin against his.

As soon as she slid her palm against his, he felt tingles of excitement coursing through him. This was a first. He gave her hand a gentle squeeze as he looked down at her staring up at him. He could not help but think she seemed so trusting, he did not want to hurt her ever.

"Aren't we going riding?"

"What? Oh, yes. Right this way." Randy blinked stupidly before turning toward the stairs. He led her over to the passenger side of the Mule before running around the back to get to the driver's side. They sped away toward the stables.

BECKY SINCERELY HOPED she would not make a fool of herself with her horse handling skills. While she had been an avid rider as a kid, it had been many years since she had been riding. As they drove closer to the stables, her nerves began to kick into high gear.

Deciding to fess up, she said, "It's been a long time since I've ridden."

"No worries. It's just like riding a bike. I'm sure you'll do fine." Randy came to a stop outside the building, and turned to smile at her.

She felt her heartbeat quicken at the look he gave her. Never before had she seen him look at Katy this way, it must be something new just for her. That thought seemed just as disturbing as the idea of thinking about Katy at all in this moment.

Becky merely nodded and let herself out of the four-wheeler. Taking a deep, calming breath, she stepped toward the breezeway, already seeing the groom holding the reins to two large horses. Randy stepped up behind her, his hand pressing gently on the small of her back as if to propel her forward.

Every time he touched her, it almost made her mind go blank. Just the thrill of him being near was enough to make her blush, but that was impractical when she was working in the kitchen. Now, she was in his domain, and she was about to go riding alone with him.

The darkness provided her some measure of privacy, but she was still going to be spending several hours alone with him. Her mind was still dallying along these lines when her feet suddenly left the ground. Instantly, her attention came back to the present as she squealed, "What're you doing?" Her arms immediately wrapped around Randy's neck as she clung to him as if her life depended on it.

Feeling the rumble of his chest against her side, she knew

he was chuckling at her reaction. The next thing she knew, she was being thrust up onto the horse's back and Randy was standing on a mounting stool next to her. He patted her knee and said, "I didn't have all day for you to decide to get mounted. I thought I'd give you a hand."

Even as he spoke, his hand rested on her knee closest to him. She felt the warmth of his fingers through the denim of her jeans and she rather liked it. Randy made her feel safe, like she could take a chance with him and she would be okay.

"All you had to do was ask, you know." Becky knew she sounded surly, but he had caught her by surprise. She picked up the horse's reins and adjusted them until they fit in her fingers as she had been taught so long ago. Maybe Randy was right with his bike riding analogy.

"Let me fix those stirrups for you," Randy offered.

"If I didn't know better, I'd think you were trying to make up for manhandling me," she teased, even as she pulled her foot forward to allow Randy ample space for making the adjustment.

"Manhandling? That's what you got out of that? I thought I was being extremely gentle. After all, I could've just thrown you over my shoulder and thrown you over the horse's back on your belly."

"Oh, well if that's your measure of gentleness, then I guess I'm grateful for the treatment I got." Randy grabbed her heel and put her foot in the stirrup.

He looked up and asked, "How does that feel?"

Becky tested the fit and answered, "Perfect."

The groom stepped forward and effortlessly adjusted the other stirrup to the same level. Becky noticed how the groom managed to make the change without ever having to touch her. It made her realize the difference between Randy's personalized attention versus the professionalism of the groom. She decided she much preferred Randy's style.

"I think I'm all set," Becky commented, ready to get away from the stables and see the countryside as Randy always spoke of it.

Randy strode away from her side and easily mounted his horse. With practiced ease, he turned his horse around until he could see her head-on as he said, "Let's get riding then. I've got lots to show you."

Becky could see his grin in the light of the moon as well as hear it in the tone of his voice. She liked how he seemed to be having a good time after so many weeks of stress. She wished she would have thought of taking a horse ride earlier. Although, he might have created a negative association with the activity had it been too soon after the news of his parents' disappearance.

"Let's get moving then. I can't wait to see it all." Becky tapped the horse's sides with her heels while clicking her tongue. Yep, it was all coming back to her with ease.

Randy's lead lessened as he slowed his horse enough for Becky to come up beside him. The horses obviously knew one another well as they paced themselves as if they were attached to a wagon. Becky let her body move to the motion of the horse's gait and silently took in Randy's running commentary about the ranch.

CHAPTER 14

While the daytime temperature had been well into the eighties, the setting of the sun also brought cooler breezes. Soon, even the riding was not enough to keep them warm as the temperature dropped into the high fifties. When Randy noticed Becky trying to hide her shivers, he pulled his horse to a stop near a spindly tree.

"Why're we stopping?"

"This's one of my favorite places to hang out as a kid. Come on down and I'll show you why." Randy looked up at her with a silly grin on his face.

"Okay," Becky said slowly as she brought her leg around the back of the horse. As soon as she dropped to the ground, her legs seemed to give out.

Randy swiftly moved beside her to hold her upright until she could get her land legs back. "I didn't think about the fact that your first ride in years would be hard on you. I'm sorry, that was thoughtless of me. Sit down over here and we can rest for a while." He led her over to a large, flat rock and helped her settle herself.

Within minutes, he had stacked the kindling inside his childhood fire-ring. With practiced ease, he got the flames licking at the dry wood as he stacked larger chunks of the fragrant hickory wood onto the small inferno.

Satisfied that he had stoked it enough to last for at least an hour, he moved to sit down next to Becky. Resting his shoulder against her leg, he leaned back on her boulder and stretched out his feet toward the flames. Wanting to be able to easily look at Becky, he removed his cowboy hat and placed it across his lap.

"Does that feel better yet?" He glanced up at her, a small smile playing across his lips. If it were even possible, she looked even more beautiful in the light of the fire. Something about the play of the flames in her eyes made him think she was more mysterious than ever. He had a sudden urge to know everything about her.

"Yes, thank you." Becky leaned forward, her hands outstretched toward the welcome heat. A small groan escaped her lips.

"A bit sore, huh?"

"Oh, you think? I doubt I'll be able to stand tomorrow."

Randy chuckled. "Tell me more about the things you like doing."

"Like what?"

"I don't know. Is there anything you've wanted to try but never had the chance to get around to?"

Becky tilted her head as she considered his question. "I've always had my music and I learned to ride when I was young. Let's see. I guess I've always wanted to go flying."

"Like in an airplane or a helicopter?"

"Either. I've never been in the air before so I don't know what either experience is like."

"Never? Well, we'll have to change that. I'll have Hector take us flying tomorrow."

"Oh, I'm sure you've got more important things to do than entertain me."

"Nope. I can't think of anything I'd rather do than experience your first flight."

Becky chuckled lightly but remained silent.

"What else."

"I'm almost afraid to say anything."

"Why?"

"Because then you'll make arrangements for whatever it is."

"What's wrong with that?"

"Um, I'm your employee, for one. What'll people say if you start making special compensations for me?"

"I don't care."

"I do."

Randy fell silent as he thought about how to fix this situation. He wanted Becky to feel special, he wanted to make things happen for her. But he also didn't want to make her feel uncomfortable.

Feeling anxious to make things right, Randy jumped up from where he sat so he could rummage through his horse's saddle bag. Finding what he knew the groom would include, he pulled the pouch out and returned to the fire. "Are you hungry? I've got the perfect trail food." He handed her a piece of jerky as he sat next to her on the stone. "This is from our beef here on the ranch."

Becky took the offering and bit into it. "Mmm. This's good. Is that hickory smoke flavoring?"

"Not flavoring, it's the real thing. We smoke it here as well. I've always loved eating this."

"Well, we're not exactly on a trail ride."

"Close enough. About that...," he paused to chew on another bite of jerky.

"About what?" Becky turned to face him, her jerky forgotten in her hand as it rested in her lap. Her eyes narrowed as she tried to figure out where he was going with this conversation.

"I can see I have you curious," Randy said as he chuckled at her expression. "Well, in the olden days, we would ride out on the trail to look out for the cattle and check the fence lines. Any more, we use the helicopter. It's time for us to do another inspection and I thought you might like to go along for the ride."

Becky's mouth thinned as her eyes narrowed suspiciously. "Right. The timing is a bit suspect."

"Seriously, Becky. Almost every worker here at the ranch has gone for rides in the helicopter." Seeing Becky begin to shake her head in denial, he added swiftly, "Even Mabel has gone up on a couple occasions."

"Really? Even Mabel. How come I'm having a hard time believing that?"

"No, it's true. You can ask her when we get back. I can think of the first time, Cookie ran out of his special seasoning while we were out. He called it in and asked Mabel to bring it to him. He wouldn't trust anyone else with the secret ingredient."

"Cookie? Who's that?"

"Oh, it's just Jacob. When he's running the chuck wagon, he insists we all call him Cookie."

Becky chuckled, "I see. And the other times Mabel went?"

"She discovered her love for flying on that first day. Since then, she's asked to go whenever her schedule would allow it."

"Wow! Who would've thought?"

"I know. Mabel's full of surprises. She's the best."

"I quite agree." Becky resumed eating her jerky while staring at the fire flickering in the breeze. "So when would you be planning the flight?"

"Tomorrow."

"Hmm. Tomorrow. Isn't that the same day you said you'd arrange for Hector to take me flying?"

"The very same. Look, Becky, I want to do something nice for you, but if you insist on making it complicated, then you're just going to have to go along with how I solve the problems you come up with."

"Oh, I have to go along, do I?"

Randy bit his cheek, wondering what made him blurt it out so wrong. Hearing her defensive tone caused him considerable worry until he saw the smirk beginning to form on her lips. He seemed to be paying a lot of attention to her lips lately. "Yes."

"What else will I have to go along with? Are you going to make a habit of this with me?"

"Only if you keep trying to say no to me."

"Hmm. We'll just have to see about that."

"Hey, that wasn't an invitation for you to try to avoid my gifts."

"Gifts? You mean there's more?" Becky stared at him, her eyes wide with concern.

"Many. And I'll keep giving them to you until you make it easier on me. We'll turn it into a habit yet."

"Goodness. What've I gotten myself into with you? My life used to be so simple before we met."

"I can simplify it even more if you'd let me."

"Oh? How would you accomplish that?"

Randy drew his pinched thumb and index finger across his pursed lips and mimed throwing the key away. "Nope. My lips are sealed. No hints. You'll just have to find out."

"You're too much, Randy." Becky turned back toward the fire.

They sat in silence for some time, enjoying the noises of the night and the crackling of the fire. More than once, they spotted a falling star in the clear evening sky. It turned out to be a perfect evening to soothe Randy's soul.

Feeling as if he had won a small victory with the fact she had not simply refused to accept any gifts, he casually put his arm around her shoulders. He drew her unresisting body close to his chest as he leaned over her head. Taking a deep breath, he could smell her apple scented shampoo mixed with the hickory smoke from the fire. To him it was ambrosia. She could not have worn a more perfect mixture of scents if she had planned it.

"What're you thinking, Randy?"

"That you smell amazing." He drew in another loud breath through his nose as if to tease her.

"You can't be serious. I probably smell like horses and dust."

"Not at all. You're all apples and hickory smoke. But there's nothing wrong with horses and trail dust either."

Becky's shoulders shook with her silent chuckling. "Only you would find that attractive."

"You wear it well. I might have to make a perfume with those scents so I can always remember this first night alone with you."

"What would you call it?"

"Let's see. How about Summer Love?"

"A bit presumptuous, don't you think?"

"Maybe a little." Randy pulled her closer to him as he planted a kiss on the top of her head. "The fire's starting to die down. Are you ready to head back?"

"Sure. Although, I'm not sure how I'm going to get back on that horse. My legs are already growling at me for the treatment they've received."

"Oh, that's easy. I'll just pick you up like I did back at the stables."

"Oh, no you won't. You had the step to help you that time. I don't see any step out here."

"Fine. But you're wrong about the step. What do you think you're sitting on?" He patted the stone next to him as he teased her a little more.

"Genius. I might just manage if you can hold my horse for me."

"Donas."

"What?"

"Your horse's name is Donas."

"Of course. I don't know why I didn't think to ask what his name was. Wait? Does that mean devil?"

Randy laughed as he stood up to begin kicking dirt over

the remnants of the fire. "Yes. He was quite the devil when we were first training him. But he's turned out to be one of our most gentle mounts. It's why I requested him for you. He has a very smooth gait and a good temper."

"I quite agree."

Stamping across where the fire had resided, Randy made sure to extinguish all of the active coals before he could be satisfied that they were ready to leave. He brushed off his jeans as he strode over to where he had tied the horses' reins to the scrubby tree behind them. Leading Donas back to stand next to the rock they had used as their seat, he said, "Your mount, my lady."

"You're too kind," she answered playfully. She groaned as she hoisted herself up onto the rock. "I'm going to pay for this tomorrow."

"But it was worth it. Right?" Randy asked, suddenly concerned she might refuse another ride in the future if this became too uncomfortable. After she seated herself, he came to stand next to her knee while he handed her the reins. He stared into her face, waiting for her answer which was slow to come.

"Definitely worth it, Randy. I think we might have to take shorter rides until I can get back into riding shape, though."

"I think I can arrange that as well." He did not bother trying to hide his grin of pleasure at her answer. He turned and easily mounted his horse before clicking his tongue to get both mounts to move out of camp and head back toward home.

CHAPTER 15

Another song began forming in her mind even before she was fully awake. Since this was a common occurrence, she reached for her phone beside the bed and pressed the record button on her voice recording app to capture the gist of the tune before it escaped her. Nothing frustrated her more than thinking she would remember it and take time to get ready for the morning only to discover it completely escaped her mind, never to return again.

This song brought a smile to her lips as its primary focus was on Randy and their ride through the dark prairie. She wondered if the thrill of the company created the magical ambiance or if it were the fireflies and shooting stars that made it so special. In either event, she was thankful for the night out.

If only it could be my forever life, she thought to herself as she pressed stop on the recorder. Rolling over on her bed, she noticed it was nearly seven and close enough to the time for her to get up that she may just as well do it. She flipped the covers back and pushed herself up into a sitting position at the edge of her bed.

Her worst fears were realized. Every part of her body ached from the trail ride. Maybe twirling around in a hot shower would help to loosen her up. *It better*, she thought, *or else I won't be much help to Mabel in the kitchen this evening.*

After her thirty-minute shower, she finally made an appearance in the kitchen. One look at Mabel's face let her know the old woman knew exactly how she felt. She grimaced as she made slow progress across the expansive kitchen.

"I put some painkillers and water on the counter for you," she said as she picked up her coffee and drank. The mischievous sparkle in her eyes made its appearance over the rim of her cup even though she never said a word.

"If only this would cure all of my aches," Becky moaned. After swallowing, she went to the coffee maker and poured herself a cup before joining Mabel at the barstools. "Randy tells me you've gone flying in the helicopter. Is that true?"

"Yes. Almost everyone here goes at least once. Why does that surprise you?"

Becky shrugged. "You just don't come across as someone who wants to leave the Earth for a joyride."

"I thought you already knew I'm full of surprises." Mabel quirked her eyebrow, and one side of her mouth tipped up at the corner.

"True. Randy asked me to go up today. I'm not sure I'll manage to get into the helicopter if I can't lift my legs."

"You're going to love it. Are you going to check the fences or count the cattle?"

"I think he mentioned something—"

"Definitely the fence lines," Randy interrupted the conversation as he strode confidently into the kitchen and walked straight for the coffee machine. "Is this a new blend? It smells amazing."

"It's peppermint mocha. If you don't like it, I'll brew you a fresh batch of your regular," Mabel offered, although she did not bother to move from her seat. "You're up earlier than normal. I haven't even started breakfast."

Randy turned while sipping his coffee. "Mmm, this's good. Yeah, my eyes popped open this morning, and I just couldn't imagine staying in bed a moment longer. I hope you don't mind me invading your space so early." He crossed the room and took the bar stool next to Becky.

"You know I always enjoy your company," Mabel replied, keeping her eyes focused on the morning paper.

"And how about you, Becky? How're you feeling this morning?" Randy asked a little too innocently.

"Like I got hit by a truck." She grinned before amending her statement, "Or maybe one of your prize steers ran me over. I'm not sure I'll be up for taking that flight."

"You'll do fine. I'll make sure you have a great time."

"Really? How do you plan to do that?"

"You have to ask? Ouch. I'll be going with you; that should be enough to make it great."

"Confident much?" Becky playfully shook her head. "Seriously, I'm looking forward to the experience. I just hope I don't get airsick."

"Not many people do with Hector flying. He's an amazing

pilot. I scheduled the flight for nine o'clock. Is that going to work?"

"Nine? Good grief, we're going to have to hustle to get your breakfast ready." Becky set her coffee cup down hard enough for the hot liquid to splash over the edge onto her thumb. She hastily stood, ready to charge into action, cringing at the sudden movement, but determined to hide her disability.

"There's no rush, Becky. Besides, I think I just want flap-jacks and eggs. Nothing fancy today." He stood and followed her around the island, his gait smooth and sexy. The hours of riding didn't seem to bother him at all. "I'll even help."

Becky eyed him suspiciously before saying, "I'm not sure how much help you'll actually be. Maybe you should sit and help Mabel with her crossword."

"I'm good," Mabel commented.

Restraining herself from glaring at Mabel's defection from helping with Randy, Becky turned her attention to gathering supplies for making the flapjacks, making sure to get the pan on the stove heating so it would be hot when the batter was ready. As soon as her hand reached out for the mixing bowl, her fingers made contact with Randy's. Immediately, she pulled back as if electrocuted. In fact, it felt just like that to her.

With wide eyes, she glanced up to see Randy grinning back at her. He seemed oblivious to what she just experienced, yet he picked up the bowl and offered it to her. "Did you want this?"

"Yes. Thank you," she replied, careful to avoid contact again as she plucked the bowl out of his hand. With more purpose than before, she focused her attention solely on making the meal. If she allowed her mind to wander over the past few minutes, then she was afraid she would forget an ingredient and spoil the breakfast.

"Are you nervous?" Randy asked, handing her the salt as he leaned against the counter beside her workspace.

She measured in the salt and mixed it by hand. She poured in cold buttermilk and gave the bowl's contents a final stir. She carefully spooned the mixture into the hot frying pan before turning to face Randy. "Maybe a little. I just don't know what to expect."

"Expect to have fun. That's all. Enjoy the view and the company."

Becky grinned as she looked up at him. She grabbed the towel and wiped her hands before swiping it across the counter. "Yes, I've always liked Hector." She took pleasure in seeing him look slightly confused before he caught on to her playful banter.

"Yes. Hector." Randy cleared his throat before pointing to the pan. "Don't those need to be turned?"

"What? Yes!" Just before the pancakes burned, she managed to flip them over. "You're too distracting. If you want your breakfast to be edible, I suggest you go visit with Mabel."

He leaned his hip against the countertop, crossed his arms over his chest, and roguishly grinned. "That's okay. I'll eat anything you make for me. I'm not picky."

"I can attest to that," Mabel piped in. "You should've seen some of the things Randy ate while out on the trail when he was little."

Becky raised an eyebrow toward Mabel as she scooped

the finished pancakes out of the pan onto the warming plate. "Do tell."

"I think we've heard enough," Randy interrupted, reaching across Becky to grab up the plate.

Becky slapped his hands away as he continued to fuss with the flapjack's placement. "Oh, no. I'd like to hear this."

"I used to lick the cow lick, okay?"

The spoon froze mid-pour, and she stared at Randy. "Ew! What made you want to do that?"

Randy shrugged as he reached into the cupboard to get the maple syrup. "I don't know. I guess I wanted to know what made the cows so interested in it."

"And?"

"It's salty."

The group laughed while Becky whipped up a dozen eggs in another bowl. She poured the mixture into the hot pan and stirred them lightly until they were fluffy and ready. Picking up the pan, she upended some of the contents on everyone's plates that Randy supplied while she had her back turned.

"Will you stop teasing me, Becky? I might starve to death over here," Randy announced.

She rather liked stalling, especially when she kept learning interesting tidbits about this man who captured her interest. Her culinary instructor would have a conniption fit if he found out she served breakfast without any embellishments, but this was a working ranch. Those kinds of frivolous touches went unnoticed anyway.

She handed Randy two of the dishes and picked up the third for herself. Becky followed Randy to the barstools at the island and seated herself at the end, letting Randy sit between herself and Mabel.

No sooner did she get situated than Mabel folded her paper and stood. "I'm going to take mine into my room. There's a new weatherman on the morning show, and I don't want to miss him."

Becky's eyes narrowed at Mabel's retreating back.

Randy picked up his fork and said, "I guess we get to keep each other company. Unless you have plans as well."

"I do have a new song to write down, but I can stay for a few more minutes."

"I'd like to hear it. Maybe you should work on it out here." He glanced at his watch and added, "It'll be nine o'clock before we know it, and we'll have to leave."

She paused with her first bite of flapjacks ready to enter her mouth. "Why did you have to remind me? Maybe I shouldn't eat before we go." She lowered her fork, forlornly looking at the breakfast and reappraising the risk.

"Trust me. You'll be fine. Let's enjoy the meal." He held out his forkful toward her, waiting for her to finish the toast.

Grinning, she tapped her fork against his and said, "To flapjacks, coffee, and good company." She took the first bite, relieved to find it every bit as delicious as the pancakes she made in culinary school.

Randy's grin widened, and he lifted his fork higher. "And to fun flights." He shoved the massive bite into his mouth. Within seconds, he theatrically rolled his eyes and mumbled, "These are the best flapjacks I've ever eaten." He swallowed and leaned closer. "Just don't tell Mabel I said that."

Becky's gaze flicked toward the hallway off the kitchen. Mabel's room must have paper-thin walls since she always heard everything. But, since no retort came from the kind, old woman, Becky leaned until her shoulder brushed against his and whispered, "Your secret's safe with me."

THE DIFFERENCE between seeing the helicopter from a distance and standing feet away left Becky with a flutter in her stomach. She was really going to fly for the first time. Looking over at Randy's confident expression and the smile he reserved just for her, she squared her shoulders to the journey.

She took Randy's hand as he helped her into the wide opening. Taking the seat farthest away from the opening, she watched as Randy pulled himself into the luxurious craft. For some reason, she expected it to be a little more rustic inside, so the plush interior helped her to relax.

"Are you ready?" Randy held out his hand for her to hold onto during the flight.

"Ready as I'll ever be," Becky replied, forcing a tremulous smile onto her lips.

Randy nodded as he spoke to Hector about the route they would take.

Becky liked the feeling of his calloused hand holding hers. They touched one another casually while they were cooking, but this time felt different. He didn't have a reason to continue to touch her except for the sheer desire to comfort her, and she liked it. Part of her mind kept preoccupied with this new experience, so she missed out on the rotors beginning to turn.

Randy held out a headset to her, breaking her concentration. Startled out of her reverie, she took the strange headset and plunked it onto her head.

Again, Randy took the liberty to adjust the microphone, so it almost touched her mouth, his fingers accidentally brushing her bottom lip as he did so. Becky resisted the urge to bite her lip in her embarrassment of the seemingly intimate contact.

"Can you hear me okay?" Randy's voice sounded directly into the ear pieces of the headset.

Becky nodded.

"Answer me out loud so we can adjust the volume of your mic," Randy insisted.

"Yes. I can hear you just fine." Becky thought it odd to hear her own voice sounding hollow to her ears. By now, the rotors had reached full power, and they were ready to go.

Hector announced, "If everyone's buckled in, then we'll be taking off."

Randy looked down at both of their seatbelts before he said, "Here we go."

Becky's gaze redirected itself until she stared out at the swiftly receding ground as the helicopter lifted vertically before tipping forward slightly as they began floating along. Randy truly spoke when he bragged of Hector's flying skills. She hardly noticed her body shifting as they changed directions to follow the fence line leading away from the stables into the countryside Becky had yet to see.

Randy kept a running commentary of the varying landscape they traversed. On more than one occasion, he told of funny adventures he encountered as a kid on the trail with Cookie. Hearing him talk about himself as the Little Mary caused Becky to look at him with a quizzical expression.

"It's just a title given to the person assigned to be Cookie's lackey. I pretty much had to do anything he told me to do, like peel potatoes or scrub out the pots in the creek. Not very glorious, but I never complained. I loved being out on the trail with the guys."

"I imagine that would seem like quite the adventure to a little kid. How old were you the first time you went out?"

"I must've been about three or four when I came out for the first time with Pop. It wasn't until I was about eight before Mom would let me come out here without him. I still remember feeling so cool with my new riding gear and strutting across the yard while waiting for the men to get ready to leave."

"I bet you were cute." Becky smiled at the vision of him in her head.

"Yeah, but my smile only lasted the first couple of hours. Nobody told me that new gear was a bad idea for a long ride. I was so sore. After that time, I wore my riding gear outside whenever I played so they'd get properly worn in and I could enjoy the trail with the rest of the guys."

"How long were you the Little Mary?"

"Until I was old enough to prove myself as the night hawk."

"What's that?" Becky looked away from the vista view to look back at Randy.

"A fancy title for someone riding the outskirts of the herd all night long to keep them safe."

"Oh, alone in the dark. How old were you?"

"Ten." Randy grinned in memory of that time. "I wanted to be younger than Pop said he was when he first did night hawk duty. I was scared to death and dog tired the next morning, but I did it. I didn't realize that proving myself only offered my nightly services for the remainder of the trail ride. I almost fell out of my saddle on more than one occasion as I nodded off to sleep during the day."

"Oh, that's terrible."

"Nah. Pop assured me that it was character-building. Besides, the trail hands treated me with more respect after that. I wasn't just the boss's son; I was one of them. I loved it all."

"What other jobs did you do?"

"Everything, really. Now I'm just Ranny."

"Ranny?"

Randy chuckled at the nickname. "It's pretty appropriate considering my real name. It's the shortened title for the Ranahan, which they give to the top cowhand."

Becky suddenly became distracted when the helicopter made an abrupt change. She whipped her head around to stare outside the window, only to discover they had landed. "What's wrong? Why did we land?"

"Easy, Becky. Nothing's wrong. I have a surprise for you. C'mon, let's go for a walk outside." Randy pulled on her hand, which he managed to keep holding for the duration of the flight.

Using her free hand, she unbuckled her seat belt and followed after Randy. She didn't know when he would have found time to arrange a surprise, but she was excited to find out what it could be. Stepping out onto the hard-packed dirt, she looked around expectantly. Only the rolling landscape surrounded them; nothing seemed out of the ordinary.

Turning her gaze toward Randy, she said, "I don't understand."

"You will shortly. C'mon!" Randy pulled her away from the helicopter, where Hector sat with a grin on his face.

Whatever was going to happen, Hector seemed to be in on it. Shaking her head in dismay, Becky blindly followed Randy. She had no idea what to expect, but she was game to find out.

CHAPTER 16

Randy's paces lengthened until he realized how hard he was pushing Becky to keep up with him. His pleasure in the anticipation of his surprise made him want to get her reaction faster. When they came over the top of the hill, he paused to wait for her reaction.

"What's this? Where did this come from?" Becky asked, her eyes lighting up and a smile tugging at her lips.

"I wanted us to have a private picnic. C'mon; let's go sit down." He tugged her hand again, noticing she came along with him readily. "You probably didn't realize how long we've been flying, but I'm hungry and I hope you are, too."

Becky glanced down at her watch, her mouth rounding in astonishment at the hours which had passed. Even as she glanced back up at him, her stomach growled. "I guess I'm hungry, too!"

Laughing, they took the last few steps until they reached the red and white checked blanket where a basket sat in the middle of it. Randy settled her down on a couple of pillows before sitting opposite her on his own pillows. Reaching forward, he pulled the wicker basket closer to him and opened one side.

Soon, the spread of food sat out on the blanket around them. Randy handed Becky a plate and said, "Take whatever you like. There's enough for an army here."

"I should say! Where'd all this come from? I don't recall seeing Mabel making anything extra."

"Nope. Mabel suggested I let you sample Cookie's mastery of trail food."

With her eyebrows high, she looked back down to the food, her appreciation evident in her expression. "This's how you eat on the trail?"

"What? No! Definitely not. Cookie wanted to show off a little. Here, try this." He picked up a beef rib and held it out toward her. "It's still warm from the smoker."

Becky held out her plate, eager to sample the famous ribs again. On one other occasion, she had been honored to try the recipe, but it was after it had already grown cold.

"He wanted to welcome you to the ranch."

"I've already been welcomed."

"Not as my girlfriend."

Becky's hand stopped on its way up to her mouth. Her eyes widened as she asked, "Is that what this's about? You laying your claim on me in front of all of the ranch hands?"

"Not exactly. But I did want to let you know that I really like being with you. I didn't know I could feel this easy with anyone."

"I think you need more time. After all, Katy has only barely left. Didn't you tell Mabel that you were going to ask

Katy to marry you just after you arrived here? I don't want to be your rebound."

Shaking his head in denial, Randy rushed to add, "I'm not rebounding. You've been here for me since the moment I discovered my parents were missing. Katy didn't even have time to call and ask me if I were doing okay."

"I was only doing the right thing, Randy. That doesn't make me special."

"Yes, it does. It makes you a caring person who happens to love ranch living as much as I do. Don't you see? You and I have so much in common; way more than Katy and I have ever had. I only imagined I could be happy with her. I had to constantly work on it. There were so many things I had to overlook with Katy.

"With you, it's as easy as breathing. I don't have to struggle to word things correctly. Goodness knows, I've bungled up so many things with you, but you just laughed it off and understood my intention.

"That never would've happened with Katy. She'd be giving me the silent treatment and making me work at getting back in her good graces. To be honest, being with Katy was exhausting."

Taking a bite of the rib, Becky listened to Randy speak his mind. When he paused for a few seconds, she wiped her lips with the linen napkin and said, "I'm glad to know I'm so easy." A smile tweaked the edges of her mouth.

"I didn't say you were easy," Randy rushed to say. Only after he looked at Becky's eyes did he notice she was only teasing him. "There, you see? You're making a joke out of my bungled words. Katy never joked. Life was always so serious for her."

"Great now I'm easy and funny. Two traits I've always aspired to in my life."

"I give up," Randy replied, chuckling as he began digging into Cookie's delicious dishes.

"I hope you didn't come all this way just so we could talk about Katy."

"Definitely not. I'm sorry I brought her up at all. I wanted to know more about you. What makes you happy? What I can do to make you happier?"

"I'm already happy. I've got a dream job at a dream location and I've got my music."

Feeling a prickle of pain at her lack of mentioning a relationship with him, he pressed the issue a bit. "I didn't hear you say anything about having a relationship. Isn't that something you're interested in?"

Becky stared down at her plate for a few seconds, her expression remaining pensive. Finally, she looked up and answered, "I have a hard time with that aspect."

"Why?" Randy's response seemed to blurt out of his mouth without giving any conscious thought that she might not want to share. Instantly regretting his rash reply, he opened his mouth to take it back when Becky started talking again.

"I guess it's only fair that I tell you what's keeping me distant." She set her plate down on the blanket between them, her face tilted down as her hair swung forward as if to hide herself from him.

Randy wanted to tell her it did not matter, that she could keep her secret. He hated thinking this conversation would cause her any pain. Yet, he desperately wanted to know why she resisted her desire to be with him. At least he thought he could tell she liked being with him. Suddenly, he felt so insecure about the whole thing.

"I told you before that my mother died when I was a little kid." She fiddled with the edge of the blanket, keeping herself closed off from him.

Not wanting to keep her from continuing, he simply made a small noise of affirmation.

"What I didn't tell you was about the argument I overheard them having before she drove away." This time, Becky did look up to look him straight in the eyes. "My mother found out that my father cheated on her. She wanted him to deny it, but he didn't. She screamed at him and rushed forward to hit him on the chest.

"He didn't even try to defend himself against her anger. When she turned around and rushed out of the house, he still didn't do anything to try to stop her. I saw her face right before she left the driveway.

"You see, I ran into the living room and watched her leave. Never dreaming that it'd be the last time I saw her. Several hours later, the police showed up at the house to deliver the news that she had hit a telephone pole and died instantly.

"From that day on, I never forgave my dad for killing my mom. She never would've been driving if it hadn't been for him cheating on her."

"Becky," Randy reached out and touched her hand where it rested on the blanket between them. "I'm so sorry. I'm sure that was a terrible burden to carry all of these years."

"Yes," Becky pulled her hand away, lifting it up to brush the tears away from her cheeks. "I don't know why it still makes me cry. It's just ridiculous."

"No, Becky, it's not ridiculous. Never feel bad about showing your emotions. It's one of the things I love about you."

"You don't even know me, Randy. You can't possibly love me."

"What I do know about you I love. Is that hard for you to hear?"

Taking a deep breath, Becky nodded and answered, "Maybe. Besides, it feels like you're just trading Katy for me and I don't want to be the other woman. That's what hurt my family in the first place. I don't want that for myself."

Randy scooted closer to her, shaking his head in denial of her statement. "No, Becky. It's not true. We already talked about this. You and Katy are nothing alike. I didn't know how selfish she was until after my parents..." His throat closed up, preventing him from finishing his sentence.

The feeling of loneliness overwhelmed him. The realization of his parents' death seemed to hit him at the strangest times, making it hard for him to know when he was going to break down and lose control. This seemed like the worst possible time. What would Becky think of him bursting into tears out of the blue?

The warmth of Becky's hand seeped through the denim of his jeans where she rested her palm against it. "Randy, it's okay to be sad about your parents. It's all so fresh in your life. Heck, I cry over my mom still and it's been over fifteen years. It's not something you ever 'get over,' but I promise it does get easier to remember the good times rather than their loss."

Another sob tore through him before he finally managed to rein in his emotions. It made him feel better knowing

Becky understood what he was going through, but he wished she had not had to witness his weakness. "I'm sorry."

"Don't be. I'm glad to see you letting the emotions out. It's really bad to keep them bundled up inside of you. I don't ever want you to hold in anything you're feeling when you're around me. Do I make myself clear?" Becky patted his leg playfully.

Opening his eyes, his blurred vision took in Becky's smile. More than anything he wished he could just take her in his arms and kiss her until they were both breathless. His eyes pled with her to make the first move, but she remained still, merely looking back at him with concern written all over her face.

Not able to stand it any longer, he leaned over onto his fists and hoisted himself up. "Let's go for a walk."

"Okay," Becky replied readily. Her tone sounded a little uncertain, but she went along with his suggestion without any complaint.

CHAPTER 17

The stark landscape seemed to soothe their souls as they walked side-by-side. Becky kept glancing over toward Randy trying to gauge his mood. Judging by his posture, she guessed he was getting his emotional bearings again.

"What are your long-term plans for the ranch?" Becky asked softly.

"I think I'm going to give up my apartment in Houston and live here full-time." He scuffed his feet along the dry soil, causing small puffs of dust to rise up in front of them.

"How much of that decision is based on getting away from Katy?"

"I thought we were done talking about her."

"Is that your way of avoiding my question?"

A smile quirked the side of his mouth but he answered playfully, "Maybe."

"At least you're being honest with me." Becky wished

Katy did not even have to be something they would have to discuss, but it was naive to think otherwise.

"I'll always be honest with you, Becky. It's the way I was raised. What about you? What're your plans? Surely you don't want to be a cook for the rest of your life."

"I'm not a cook. I'm a chef."

"Is there a difference?" Randy stopped walking next to a pile of rocks and faced her, his expression earnest in his desire to understand.

"Of course. It's like saying that a Quarter horse is the same as a thoroughbred." Becky squinted up at him where the sun shone brightly just to the side of his head.

Quirking one eyebrow, he tilted his head to the side and drawled, "Why didn't you say that before?"

"I didn't think I had to. It seems so obvious to me."

"So tell me what the difference really is." Randy looked down at the boulders and decided to seat himself on one large enough for them to share.

Taking a moment to compose her thoughts as she seated herself next to him, she finally answered, "I guess I think a cook is someone who creates meals which are standard. A chef thinks about variations of common meals and turns them into something of an art form. I think about different ingredients to combine to create a flavorful masterpiece."

"So I'm hearing you say that you don't want to have to prepare repetitive meals."

"Sort of. I mean, I'll make anything you ask me to, but I enjoy the challenge of new creations. It doesn't matter if it's the seasonings or the protein, it's all a pleasure to figure out."

Randy seemed to stare at her for several seconds longer than seemed comfortable. His eyes kept staring down at her lips, causing her to draw the bottom one in between her teeth. As if in slow motion, Randy leaned forward until they were within inches of one another. "I love hearing the way you speak about your passions." The space between them lessened until they almost touched.

Becky's breath caught in her throat as she realized he meant to kiss her. She closed her eyes and felt herself being drawn closer to him. Suddenly, an exclamation of pain caused her eyes to fly open to find out what had happened. "What's wrong?" she cried out, seeing him holding his hand up close to his chest as he jumped up from the boulder.

"Get up! Get up right now! Come over here to me."

The frightened look on his face caused her to move without any conscious thought until she stood next to him. Peering a little closer, she could see his hand looked slightly puffy. "What happened? Randy, you're starting to scare me."

"I wasn't paying attention. It was stupid of me to sit down on the boulder without first checking for snakes." His face began to pale.

"What're you saying?"

"A rattlesnake bit me."

"What? What should I do? Do I need to cut it open and suck out the poison?"

Even through his pain, he chuckled at her reply. "No, that's not what you do for this. Can you take off my belt?"

Becky fumbled with the buckle, feeling awkward as she pulled on it. Knowing her face had flushed bright red seemed like the least of their concerns as she continued to tug until she had the belt removed from all the loops. "What now?"

"Make a tourniquet on my forearm. It's got to be above

the swelling and tight enough to keep the poison from traveling farther up my arm."

"Okay," Becky replied, rushing to comply with his directions. When she finished, she looked up at his face and said, "You're not looking so good, Randy. We should get back to the helicopter so we can get medical attention."

"I can't go that far. You're going to have to go alone."

"I'm not going to leave you here at the mercy of more snakes." Her eyes automatically traveled back to the pile of stones, looking so innocuous yet hiding something so deadly.

"We can get over to that little tree and then you're going to have to go as fast as you can. As far away as we are from civilization, it's going to be hard enough to get treatment fast enough."

"Randy, don't you dare die on me!" Becky's fear rose higher at his explanation of the situation. She gauged the distance for them to walk to the small scrub tree. "You could climb on my back and I could carry you over to the tree," she offered.

Another chuckle escaped Randy's lips even as he shook his head. "No, I can make it, but let's hurry."

Becky tucked herself up against his side, looping her arm around his waist as she tried to assist him as much as possible. She did not think she was helping him much, but he seemed willing to let her try. Within a minute, they had reached their destination where she made sure he was as safe as possible. "Do you have your cell phone?"

Shaking his head sadly, he replied, "I left it in the helicopter."

Letting out an exasperated breath, she merely nodded and stood up. "I'll be back before you know it."

"I'm counting on it. Tell Hector there's a clear spot to land."

"I'm on it." Becky whirled away and let her feet fly over the dusty terrain. She had not realized how far they had gone from where Hector had landed, and she worried continuously until she came to the rise where she could see the helicopter sitting over on the next ridge.

Waving her arms desperately, she hoped to catch Hector's attention enough to alert him to a problem. Unfortunately, he seemed absorbed in whatever was on the tablet in his lap. Out of breath, she pounded the glass on the door, uncertain of how to open it.

Hector looked up, his startled expression swiftly morphing into concern as he looked at her face. Reaching across the cabin, he unlatched the door and swung it open.

"We need to help Randy. He's been bitten by a rattlesnake." Becky's explanation came out in spurts of breath as she managed to suck enough air into her lungs to tell him what happened.

"Get in!" Hector's attention immediately shifted to the panel in front of him where he began shifting switches faster than she could comprehend.

The rotors began to whirl above their heads painfully slow as the motor began to warm up to the movement. Hector handed her a headset and let her adjust it herself. As soon as they were airborne, Hector turned to her and asked through the mic, "Where is he? How bad is it?"

"He's by the pile of rocks under a little scrub tree two hills over." Becky had not really planned on how she would direct him back. Being unfamiliar with the landscape, she hoped it was enough.

"I know just the place. Good job. How long ago did he get bit?"

"About fifteen minutes ago. I ran the whole way." Seeing Hector's wince, she wished she could have run faster.

"I'm calling this into the hospital. Hold on." Hector changed the frequency of the radio and spoke with someone. He explained the situation even as he flew at breakneck speed toward Randy. The call had just finished when he began lowering the craft down to the ground. "Can you help him get inside? Or do you want me to help?"

"I think you should help. He seemed pretty weak when I left him and I'm sure he's worse now."

Hector nodded and made some adjustments to the helicopter before he took off his headset and opened his door. "Watch out for the tail rotor. Show me where he's at."

Becky made a beeline for the small tree, letting out a sigh of relief at seeing Randy still alive. She rushed to his side, falling onto her knees beside him. Feeling as though she had failed him in taking so long to get help, she lifted his limp hand into her own. Noticing how cool and clammy he had turned alarmed her even further.

"Randy, I've brought Hector. We're going to get you to the hospital right away. You're going to be just fine." Becky shifted her worried gaze over to Hector, pleading him to agree with her words of encouragement. If Randy died because of her, she would never forgive herself.

"Come on, Boss. Let's get you into the chopper. I've already called ahead to the hospital. They're expecting us to arrive shortly. We don't want to be late." Putting action to his words, the man bent over and easily lifted Randy to his feet as if this were an everyday occurrence.

In short order, but what felt like an eternity, Hector had Randy strapped into the passenger seat of the helicopter where Becky situated herself right next to him. She planned on giving Hector regular updates on Randy's condition. Becky wondered what good she could actually do for either of them since no further medical help could be rendered until they reached the actual hospital.

Other than intense fear, Becky had no recollection of the flight. She never once looked away from Randy's pallid complexion to appreciate the scenery whizzing past them. Never before had she witnessed someone go from perfect health to death's door in such a short amount of time. Never before could she imagine being so scared for someone's life.

As soon as Hector set the helicopter down on the hospital's rooftop helipad, someone rushed forward and opened the passenger door. Becky hastily unlatched Randy's seat belt and then merely pushed herself flat against the seat to keep out of the trauma team's way. With practiced ease, the medical team whisked Randy away as Becky watched through the blur of tears threatening to fall from her lashes.

"Don't worry, Becky. We got him here in time." Hector awkwardly patted her knee from where he still sat in the pilot's seat.

"How can you be sure?" Becky asked, her eyes only moving to face Hector when the doors shut on the rooftop, ending her view of Randy's gurney.

"We've seen this many times. Besides, the mortality rate of rattlesnake bites is extremely low. Now, I'm not saying he doesn't have a lengthy recovery ahead of him, but he's got youth and health on his side."

"Is there someone we should be calling to notify?" Becky

glanced back toward the doors which had hidden Randy from her sight. "It seems strange that he's going to be all alone."

"He doesn't need to be alone. You could stay with him. I'm sure he'd appreciate it." Hector's attempt at keeping his expression neutral failed miserably.

Becky drew in a shaky breath before asking, "Are you sure? I mean, I don't want to overstep my place. After all, I'm just the hired help. I don't want him to think I'm shirking my duties."

"Get out of the helicopter, Becky. I need to get clear of here for any other emergencies. I'll send a car for you in a couple of hours. Meanwhile, you can keep watch over our boss and give us regular updates. I'm sure Mabel will appreciate knowing her boy is in good hands."

"Oh, Mabel should be the one to sit with Randy. Why don't we fly back and get her?"

"Becky, get out. I'll call Mabel from the air and let her know, but I'm sure she'd agree with me that you should stay with him." Hector made a shooing gesture with his hand while lowering his eyebrows in exasperation of her delayed response to leave.

Reluctantly, Becky lowered herself down to the ground before rushing away from the rotors which were gaining momentum as Hector prepared the chopper for takeoff again. Before she could change her mind, the craft lifted off and departed the vicinity. Not having any other choice, Becky moved toward the only doors available to her. She had no idea what to expect, but she would soon find out.

CHAPTER 18

Sitting in the hospital waiting room gave Becky plenty of time to doubt the reason she had stayed. Surely, Mabel would be a better visitor. If she were being honest with herself, she felt completely responsible for Randy's health. If he had not been taking her out to see the property, then he would not have been bitten by the snake.

A couple of nurses stopped nearby having an animated conversation. Something about their urgency and tone caught Becky's attention. If they were discussing Randy's condition, she wanted to be forewarned. Not wanting to intrude, she leaned slightly closer to them and listened in.

"Did you see who came in by helicopter?" the first woman spoke, her eager tone practically dripping with eagerness to spill the juicy gossip.

"No, I just came on shift. Who was it?" a second female voice asked.

"None other than Randolph Easton."

After a slight pause, the second woman asked, "Who's that?"

"Seriously? Were you born in a barn? Mr. Easton is only the most eligible bachelor in all of Texas."

"Oh. I'm not from around here. I just transferred from Oregon. What makes him so special?"

"Oh, I don't know. It could be that he's devastatingly handsome. But the fact that he just inherited billions of dollars from his parents certainly doesn't hurt."

"Wow. What brought him here?"

"Rattlesnake bite to the hand."

"Is he going to be okay?"

"Yeah, they got him here in the golden hour. His treatments are still going to take a week so we'll all have plenty of time to flirt with him. He's in that room, just past the nurse's station."

"Seriously, Danielle. That goes directly against hospital policy. We can't fraternize with the patients. We have a job to perform."

"That doesn't mean I can't be extra attentive to him," Danielle replied, her tone slightly clipped with irritation.

Becky sat back; her mind reeled with the news of Randy's financial status. She had known his family was wealthy, but she had no idea the extent of it. Surely the nurse had been exaggerating. When she had time, she would do her own research, but now she just needed to get out of the hospital.

Knowing Randy had a good prognosis, she decided she could report back to the ranch. Even as she stood up to leave, she had an idea about leaving a note for Randy to let her know what she planned. Walking over to the nurse's station, she asked the attending nurse, "Do you have some paper and a pen so I can write a note for one of the patients?"

"Sure. Let me get that for you."

Becky watched as the woman pulled a blank sheet of copy paper out of the printer. As soon as she had what she requested, she resumed her seat in the waiting room. It took her longer than she planned to find the right words to put down. Should she tell Randy how she felt responsible, or should she tell him how worried she had been for him? Maybe she should keep it professional and tell him that she had returned to her duties at the ranch.

Sighing, Becky sat back in her seat, resting her head against the white wall behind her. It did not seem like this should be so hard. Tapping the pen against the paper, Becky wondered if she were stalling because she really wanted to stay and hold his good hand while he recovered. *Of course,* she said in her head. *I'd do just about anything for him.*

Deciding these were the words she needed to put down, she leaned forward and swiftly scribbled out all of her thoughts. Starting with her excitement for the helicopter ride, segueing into her appreciation for his thoughtfulness in arranging the picnic, and then ending with her apology for not getting Hector to him sooner. The words flowed through the pen as fast as she could think them.

When she finally finished, she took another deep breath and stretched out her fingers to relieve the cramping. Usually, this type of writing only happened when she was creating a new song. She did not want to even reread the note. After folding it several times, she wrote Randy Easton on the outside so the nurses could not possibly mistake who it was meant for.

Just as she stepped away from the waiting room chair, Becky's attention shifted toward the staccato sound of high heels striking the floor. After hearing the small squeaking sounds of the nurse's shoes for the last couple of hours, this seemed totally out of place. Turning her gaze to her left, she saw a woman's elegant figure which strangely reminded her of Katy.

Shaking her head at her wild imagination, she stepped back behind the wall of the waiting room to see if her initial reaction proved true. The last thing she needed was a confrontation with that woman here in the sanctity of the hospital. After all, how would Katy even know that Randy had been admitted? It was not as if his arrival had been planned.

Within seconds, Katy's shrill voice sounded from directly ahead of her. Knowing her back would be to her, she dared to look out of her hiding place. From the designer shoes to the fancy dress, Katy looked as if she had just stepped away from a fashion photo shoot. She listened in as Katy addressed the nurse.

"I'm here to see Randolph Easton. I need to know what room he's staying in." Katy tapped her perfectly manicured nails on the Formica countertop.

"I'm sorry, he's only allowed to have family as his visitors," the nurse patiently explained.

Becky could see Katy's posture stiffen at being denied immediate access.

"Listen, you must be new around here. Randolph's parents were his only family and they just died a couple of months ago. I'm Randolph's fiancé and I'm sure he wouldn't appreciate hearing that you turned me away."

"I'm sorry, Miss. What's your name?"

This time, Becky's own spine stiffened at Katy's admission to her relationship status with Randy. Could it be true? If so, what kind of sick game was Randy playing with her? More than anything, she wanted to stomp over to Katy's side and demand to see the engagement ring.

Somehow, her feet never got the message. Deep down, she wanted to keep the answer from ever being acknowledged. As long as she could hold onto the hope of it being a lie, then she could keep letting her heart beat for Randy's love.

Another nurse stepped into the reception area, her eyes wide with recognition. "Miss Holmes, what can we help you with?"

"Finally, someone around here seems to know their job." Katy's voice could not have been more scornful if she tried. She turned her charm onto the newcomer and said, "I came to sit with my fiancé, Randolph."

"Of course. Follow me, his room is just over here."

Becky listened to the strike of the heels against the tiled floor as she left with the nurse. Deciding this would be her best opportunity to leave unseen, she scurried out of the waiting room and up to the nurse still sitting at the desk. "I'd like to leave this note for Randy Easton." She tapped it on the countertop, still holding it between her two hands.

"And what's your name?" The nurse's flushed cheeks indicated how embarrassed she had been by Katy's abominable behavior.

"Oh, I'm Becky. I work for Randy and helped bring him in on the helicopter." Seeing the nurse nod with understanding, she decided to say one last thing. She leaned forward and whispered, "Don't let Katy get to you. She's a nasty piece of work who doesn't deserve the hardworking people who work here."

The look of relief on the nurse's face made Becky wonder, once again, what had attracted Randy to Katy in the first place? His easygoing manner was a complete contrast with Katy's over-privileged attitude. She reached her hand forward and held out the note to the nurse. "Can you please make sure he gets this?"

"Certainly." The nurse took the note from her and placed it next to her keyboard, her hand patting it into place. "As soon as his visitor leaves, I'll take it to him personally."

"I'd appreciate that," Becky replied sincerely. "If he asks, will you tell him that I went back to work?"

"Sure thing."

Becky nodded before turning away from the nurse. Her feet seemed to move of their own accord as she stepped down the hallway toward the nearest exit. She hated hospitals. Ever since her mother's accident, she always dreaded the sterile scent which seemed to permeate the very walls.

As soon as she stepped outside, she inhaled the fresh air as if she had not breathed in hours. Only then did she realize she had a bigger problem; she had no way to pay for a ride home. Since she was only going for a ride on the property, she had not considered bringing her purse or even her cell phone.

She closed her eyes in disbelief as she contemplated her options. Going back inside was off limits. The very last thing she wanted was to run into Katy and receive the sharp edge of her tongue. Maybe she could find a payphone and call collect back to the ranch. Surely, Mabel would send a car for her.

"Becky?" a man's voice called out to her.

More than a little surprised at being addressed personally outside the hospital, she searched for who had spoken. Almost crying out in relief, she spotted James standing next to a Rolls Royce Phantom. "What're you doing here?" she asked, her voice going up an octave in her excitement.

"Hector said you'd need a ride home. How's Master Randy doing?"

Slapping her forehead with the palm of her hand, she recalled Hector mentioning how he would arrange transportation when he got back to the ranch. "I don't know where my head is, James. Let's get going home and I'll tell you everything I know on the way."

"Sounds good. Do you want to sit up front or in the back?" James gestured to the car.

"Up front, of course. It's not my place to sit in the back. I'm just the hired help, after all."

"If you say so," James replied cryptically. He opened her door and waited for her to seat herself.

Never before had she been in a vehicle as luxurious as this. Her hand rubbed the soft leather of the seat cushion appreciatively. Even the dull thud of the door closing made her think this vehicle had been built like a tank.

James took his seat in the driver's seat and expertly navigated his way back to the highway. "We'll be back at the ranch in a few hours."

"What?" Becky's mind reeled with the timing. "How'd you get here so fast?"

James chuckled before answering, "I was checking in with

Master Randy's business in the city when Hector called me. I only had a few things to tie up before I headed over to the hospital to get you."

"I'm sorry I kept you waiting. I'm sure you have more important things to do than hang around for me."

"No worries, Becky. I didn't wait that long. Now tell me about Master Randy's prognosis."

Once again, Becky berated herself for making this all about her rather than the more important issue of Randy's health. She spent the next half an hour explaining all that had happened during their morning outing. At the end of it, she managed to pull her hand up to her mouth just in time to cover a massive yawn.

"Go ahead and take a nap, Becky. After all, you've had quite the day so far. Besides, when you get home, I know Mabel will be pestering you for every detail you can recall. She thinks of Master Randy as her own son."

"I'm grateful for her kindness." Another yawn snuck up on her causing her to realize she needed to heed James' advice. She tucked herself against the door and closed her eyes. She never noticed James lean forward and turn on the heat to her seat, but the added warmth helped lull her into a much needed rest.

CHAPTER 19

Watching Katy saunter into the room as if she owned the place caused Randy more than a little bit of confusion. First of all, he had no idea how she knew where to find him. Secondly, he would much rather have seen Becky at his bedside.

Rather than be rude, Randy asked, "How did you know I was here?"

"Oh, Randolph! Bad news always travels at the speed of the internet."

"Ugh, really? It's already on the internet?" He shook his head in dismay. More publicity was the last thing he wanted at this point in his life. On the bright side, maybe it would change the narrative of all of the reporters from his parents' death to something more palatable.

"Don't worry, darling. I came as soon as I heard. Imagine my fear of losing you." Katy pulled up the doctor's rolling stool and seated herself at Randy's side.

He noted she avoided looking at his injured hand and

only focused on holding the uninjured one. "I'm still surprised you came. I know how you don't like hospitals."

"I actually wanted to apologize to you in person." She shifted her gaze away from him down to the edge of the bed.

"Really? What for?" Randy squeezed her hand, attempting to get her to look at him again.

As if she had read his thoughts, she stared into his eyes and said, "I've been so selfish. When your parents died, I should have been there for you. To be honest, I was just as scared for them. I had no idea how I could comfort you if I was just as much of a mess.

"So instead I kept my distance. I tried to keep myself distracted with anything I could think of just to prevent myself from having to face reality. Can you ever forgive me?"

"It's okay, Katy. I know you better than anyone in this world. I know it was hard on you, too."

A smile transformed her face instantly, as if the former conversation had never happened. "I knew you'd say that. Now, I really have to tell you what I've been up to lately. You're going to love hearing all of the stories I have to tell you about Michael."

"Ugh. What's he done now?"

Katy giggled at his reaction before she continued, "He's gotten himself a girlfriend."

"Who's the flavor of the week this time?"

"Honestly, I don't remember her name."

"Not that it matters. How long do you think she'll last?"

"I'd give it another three weeks, one month tops."

"Sounds about right." Randy wondered how often this exact game had been played between them. Always, one of his friends would get involved and they would take bets on the longevity of the relationship. More often than not, Katy would win the bet. She had an uncanny ability to see details he invariably missed. Of course, she always insisted it was her woman's intuition.

As usual, Katy changed the subject without missing a beat. "So tell me what you were doing that you found yourself becoming a snake's meal."

"Just the usual fence checking. Nothing different really. Although I should have known better than to put my hand down on a rock without first clearing the area for snakes. It was a stupid mistake that I'm not likely to forget."

"I kept telling you how dangerous it is out in the wild country. This never would've happened to you had you stayed safely in the city with me. When're you coming back to the real world, anyway?"

"The real world? Katy, I don't think you understand what's happening."

Katy's eyes narrowed as her anger flared at being contradicted. "What exactly are you saying, Randolph? Don't tell me you plan on staying out in the sticks forever."

"That's exactly what I'm saying. My parents' ranch is everything to me."

"Everything? Where does that leave us? Are you breaking up with me?"

Thinking this was the perfect opportunity to clear the air and be rid of her once and for all, he opened his mouth to speak when a knock sounded on the door. Groaning inwardly at the terrible timing, he saw the nurse enter the room.

"I'm going to have to ask you to step outside for a

moment while I examine the patient." The nurse's tone did not leave any room for argument.

Looking up at the nurse's name tag as she pulled his chart from the end of the bed, Randy suspected Danielle had plenty of practice kicking visitors out of her patients' rooms. Just this once, he wished her timing could have been delayed even one minute so he could have delivered the inevitable news to Katy.

"Fine," Katy replied cheerfully. "Randolph needs some time to decide how he wants to answer my question anyway." She stood and practically marched out of the room, her heels clicking loudly on the tiles.

"So, when's the wedding?" Danielle asked casually.

Shaking his head in confusion, Randy asked, "What wedding?"

"Why yours and Miss Holmes'."

"We're not engaged. In fact, if you hadn't interrupted us, I was just about to tell her we're through."

"Really? Well, do you need me to keep her from coming back here? After all, she did say she was your fiancé; otherwise, we never would have let her in to see you. We have a strict policy about family only when patients are first admitted."

"Ah, that explains it, then."

"I'm sorry. Explains what?"

"I expected to see Becky rather than Katy." Seeing the look of confusion on Danielle's face, he clarified, "The woman who rode with me on the helicopter."

"Oh, yes. She left a little while ago."

Feeling sorry that he had missed her he sighed deeply. Maybe he should let the nurses prevent Katy's return. At least this way, he could have more time to compose his thoughts before the fireworks of Katy's wrath came down onto his head.

FEELING her anger boiling up to the point where she thought she might explode, Katy charged out of the cramped, smelly room. She needed to find out where the cafeteria was so she could get herself a cup of coffee, although something stronger would have been her preference at this point. Seeing the desk was unoccupied, only fueled her anger further.

She leaned over the countertop, hoping to find a bell to ring for assistance. The last thing she wanted to do was wander all over this awful place just to get her caffeine fix. While she never did see a bell, she discovered something much more interesting.

With the stealth of a burglar, she picked up the paper which was addressed to her Randolph and swiftly shoved it into her clutch bag. Rather than wait around for someone to witness her appearance, she turned and headed down the hallway. She would have to locate a kiosk or another nurse to get directions.

Luckily, the first orderly to appear was a young man who seemed to appreciate her shapely body. She smiled brightly and stepped up closer than anyone would have found comfortable. "I was hoping you could assist me," she practically purred.

"Anything, Miss."

"Can you direct me to the best place to get a cup of coffee

around here?" She reached out and touched his bicep to emphasize her plight.

"I'm headed there myself. You can walk with me."

Katy barely managed to restrain herself from rolling her eyes. The last thing she wanted was someone hanging around with her in the cafeteria. The letter was practically burning a hole in her clutch and she wanted to read it.

As soon as the sign to the cafeteria became visible, Katy set her plan in action to get rid of her escort. Without any warning, she burst into tears. The idea of ruining her perfectly applied makeup caused her some distress, but the ability to get rid of her overly helpful guide seemed worth the sacrifice.

"Are you okay?" The man's expression turned mortified.

"Yes, yes. It's just I received distressing news today and it's all hitting me at once. I think I just need some time to myself. You've been so kind to help me."

"I'm sorry for your distress. Um. The cafeteria is just up this hallway." The man looked from side to side, his eagerness to get away from her quite evident.

"Thanks," her voice broke artfully on that one word as she managed to produce one tear to fall down her face. The orderly stepped aside and retreated back the way they came. She pulled a tissue out of her clutch and dabbed carefully at her face. The man had been even easier to get rid of than she originally imagined. Perhaps her makeup had survived after all.

Straightening her spine, she shook her hair back from her face as she strode confidently into the large cafeteria. She located the vending machines along the far wall and wished it could have been a coffee shop instead. Sighing with resignation, she pulled out several bills and fed them into the machine before selecting her choice of coffee.

Inhaling the bitter aroma, she turned and found a secluded table where she could have some form of privacy. At least from this vantage point, she would have plenty of warning before anyone could get close to her. She pulled out the chair, cringing at the stickiness on the seatback.

With her lip curled in disgust, she wiped her fingers on her napkin before she took her first sip of the wretched coffee. It was quite possibly the worst cup she had ever tasted. She pushed it aside and set her clutch on the table where she could extract the note.

Opening it up, she no longer cared about the coffee as the letter seemed to gush on and on about how this other woman felt about her man. When she reached the bottom and read Becky's name, she felt like screaming.

Not only had Randolph lied to her about how he had been bitten, he left out the whole part about how he had been on a date with none other than his hired help. If he thought he could get away with this betrayal, he was sadly mistaken.

Resisting the urge to crumple the note between her hands, she carefully refolded it and put it back into her purse. There was no way she would go back to Randolph's room now. She had too many ideas to put into place. Her first course of action was to plan a party; one nobody would soon forget.

CHAPTER 20

After delivering all of her news about Randy's condition to a kitchen full of concerned ranch staff, Becky excused herself to take a shower. The long ride home helped her appreciate the speed of the helicopter's transportation. The kink in her neck only proved how tired she had been after the accident.

Her mind kept replaying the scene as the water cascaded down her back as her hands held her away from the wall. More than anything, she wished the whole incident had never happened. Things between her and Randy had felt so right. She had just begun to think things could actually blossom between the two of them.

Seeing Katy saunter into the hospital only seemed to emphasize the differences between them. Katy's confidence and poise made Becky look like a wall flower by comparison. Not only that, Becky did not feel as if she were even a fraction as gorgeous as Katy. Although, the more she got to know her, the less attractive she had become.

As the water began to flow cooler, Becky realized too much time had passed while she had been contemplating her own life. With a sigh of resignation, she turned the valve to shut off the water and grabbed her plush towel to wrap around herself. She did not even bother drying her hair before making her way back to her bedroom. Just seeing her bed caused her to want to go back to sleep.

Flopping down on top of the comforter, she pulled a throw blanket over her body and closed her eyes. The first thing which came to mind was to say a prayer for Randy. She wanted him to recover swiftly and completely. If he even bore a scar from the incident, she would continue to feel guilty about the whole thing.

The last thing he needed was a permanent reminder of their disastrous date. If that's what it even was. She had almost convinced herself she had been mistaken in believing Randy felt for her the way she had begun to feel about him. There was no way he would pick her over the elegant Katy.

SOMETHING SEEMED off to Becky as she struggled to breathe. Her eyes opened slowly to notice the light had shifted in her room to indicate the whole afternoon had gone while she slept. Attempting to inhale through her nose, she realized her sinuses were completely stuffed up.

With a groan, she chastised herself for sleeping with wet hair while the air conditioner blew on her. Now she'd have to contend with a stuffy head for days on end. Feeling worse than ever, she sat up on the bed only to find a headache had developed right along with the clogged nose.

"Well, today just keeps getting better and better," she murmured to herself. Grabbing the first pieces of clothing which were within arm's length, she pulled on her sweatpants and old t-shirt before she headed back to the bathroom to see how dreadful she must look.

The mirror reflected exactly how she felt. Her skin was pale and her eyes were puffy. She could see the tightness around her mouth and eyes as she tried to keep the headache from getting worse. Even the soft light streaming in from the frosted window seemed to pierce straight through her skull. She knew the signs of a migraine and she did not have time for this.

Shielding her eyes from the light, she found her way back into the kitchen and headed straight for the medicine supply. If she could take something for the pain right away, then there was a marginal chance she could stave off the inevitable migraine. Pouring two pills into her palm, she turned to retrieve a glass of water only to discover one being held out toward her.

Recognizing the hand which held it, she said, "Thanks, Mabel." Taking the pills, she washed them down swiftly before the taste of the coating to register on her tongue.

"It looks like someone needs the rest of the day off. Why don't you let me worry about everything tonight while you head back to your room? You've had a big day."

"Thanks, Mabel. You're really the best, you know?"

"I have my moments. C'mon, let me tuck you into your bed. I'll bring you some hot broth in a few minutes."

Becky let herself be led by the arm as she kept her eyes shut. It was nice having someone who wanted to mother her; it made her miss her own mother all the more. This must be what everyone talked about when they got sick.

They entered her room where Mabel made a disapproving click of her tongue. "Well, it's no wonder you made yourself sick. Your bed is all wet. Did you fall asleep before drying off?"

"Yes. I'm sorry, Mabel. I don't want you to go to any more trouble for me." Becky's brows furrowed with distress.

"Don't you think anything of it, my girl. Just sit yourself down right here while I get you some fresh linens. I'll have you comfy in short order."

The sound of Mabel's bustling about broke the blessed silence. Within a few minutes, she said, "Now, let's get you in here."

Becky felt Mabel's warm touch on her elbow, directing her to the luxuriously soft bedding. Pulling the covers up close to her chin, Becky opened one eye enough to see Mabel still standing in her room, looking down on her with a loving expression. "Can I ask you a question?"

Mabel seated herself in the vacant chair and replied, "You know you can. Are you going to finally tell me what's been bothering you enough to worry yourself sick?"

"It's about Randy." Becky paused to formulate how to say everything she was actually thinking.

"That much was quite obvious. What about Randy?" Mabel pressed.

"I felt like things were going good between us, but then Katy showed up at the hospital and claimed to be Randy's fiancé. Now I don't know if I just misunderstood the entire day or not."

Shaking her head slowly, a small grin appeared on Mabel's face. "Love can be so blind. Listen; you've got nothing to worry about where Katy's concerned. Randy's talked my ear off about all of her shortcomings. If he really did get engaged to her, I would've been the first to hear about it.

"Randy's head over heels in love with you, Becky."

"But I'm nothing like Katy. I don't have all the fancy clothes. I'm not nearly as beautiful as her. And I definitely don't know how to dazzle people with my charm.

"He can't possibly go from her to me. Maybe I'm just a diversion, or worse, a rebound relationship." Becky rolled onto her back and threw her arm over her eyes, wishing she could just erase this day entirely.

"I don't know why you're even comparing yourself to her. That girl has as much class as a cockroach. You're more beautiful than you'll admit and you have skills that girl could only dream about."

"You're just saying that to be nice, Mabel. Don't get me wrong, I appreciate it, but just tell me straight."

"I think you've known me long enough to know I always speak the truth whether or not it's asked for. I've never lied to you and I've never even bent the truth to save your feelings. Randy wants to be with you. End of story.

"Now you think on that for a few minutes while I get some broth on the stove for you. You'll feel much more yourself once you get something in your stomach." Mabel reached out and patted Becky's forearm before leaving her alone with her racing thoughts.

Becky felt the truth in Mabel's words, but she just could not reconcile them with her own insecurities. What talents did she possess which Katy would dream about? Even the idea of it seem preposterous.

A few minutes later, Mabel returned with a tray containing the steaming bowl of broth. Becky forced herself to sit up against the headboard to allow the tray a flat spot across her lap. "That smells wonderful. What is it?"

"My special blend of spices in beef broth. I've always insisted it helps anything that ails you. Give it a try. I put a few ice cubes in it so it shouldn't burn your tongue."

Becky did as directed and sampled the liquid. As usual, her taste buds began to analyze the flavors, identifying the various ingredients.

"Quit thinking about what's in it. I'll share the recipe when you get back to yourself. Just enjoy it."

Grinning at getting caught, Becky dipped the spoon again but hesitated before taking another sip. "Can I ask you a question?"

"Anytime."

"When you said I had talents that Katy would want, what were you talking about?"

Mabel chuckled as she sat down on the chair. "Well there's your music, for one."

"Oh, Mabel. That's not a talent; it's just a hobby of mine. It's not like I'd ever make a career out of it."

"That's for you to decide, but you're definitely good enough to command a large audience. Just ask any ranch hand and they'd agree with me."

"Okay, let's table that for now. What else?"

"Your cooking, of course."

Again, Becky frowned. "That doesn't seem very important. Anybody can cook?"

"Don't let Cookie hear you say that. He'd turn you over his knee until you thought better of it."

Becky chuckled at the picture her mind created.

"Haven't you ever heard that the way to a man's heart is through his stomach?"

"Sure, but it won't make an impact in Randy's life. He could hire anyone to cook for him. Heck, he's got enough money to lure any five-star Michelin chef from any restaurant."

"He doesn't have to; he's got you."

"But Katy…"

"You know what Randy said about Katy?"

"What?"

"That the extent of Katy's experience in the kitchen is locating the takeout menus. He said she threw a fit when one of them turned up missing and he ended up going to the restaurant to get a replacement before she'd shut up about it. Can you imagine what kind of life Randy would have if he stayed with someone like that?"

Becky chuckled at the idea, yet she remained unconvinced. "It still doesn't seem like enough to dismiss their long-established relationship."

"You're forgetting the most important part."

"What's that?"

"You love this ranch as much as he does. There's no way Katy would survive out here. She's like a hothouse flower who needs to be coddled with constant attention. I've seen how you've blossomed since arriving here. This's your home, Becky."

To cover her embarrassment at Mabel's lavish praise, she lifted the spoon and filled her mouth. There was a lot to think about and she still doubted herself enough to let fear sink into her soul. "This's amazing, Mabel. Thank you."

"I'll leave you alone for now. Have a good rest, honey." She silently closed the door behind her.

Becky watched her leave, wishing with all her might she could have as much confidence. As a friend and mentor, Mabel was the best. Surely, she would not lead her astray where Randy was concerned. Hope remained a small flame inside her chest.

CHAPTER 21

Randy's homecoming was only marred by Katy's insistence at hosting a welcome home party in his honor. Luckily, she had been convinced into keeping the party small. Only Randy's closest friends and a few plus ones were invited.

Not only had she dictated what the staff should do, she brought in a full band and a decorating team to make the place look festive. Becky still winced at her idea of fashion as she batted a helium balloon out of her face as she brought another tray of hors d'oeuvres into the foyer.

She glanced at her watch and noticed it was nearly time for his car to be arriving. Her heart raced with excitement. With the guests milling through the house, she had barely had time to worry about when Randy would arrive. Now it seemed so real, so imminent that she felt a tingling all through her body at the prospect of having him back home again. Her reverie was rudely interrupted by a shrill voice sounding right next to her.

"Don't just stand there, get back to the kitchen to keep these things coming," Katy shrilled at Becky while poking her fingernail distastefully at the beef-stuffed mushrooms. "I thought I said we needed some vegan selections. All I can see is stuff made with beef."

"Exactly, Miss Holmes. Randy owns a cattle ranch and he's proud of the meat he produces. We're trying to honor him in every way we can think."

"Listen, you little tart, this's my party. You better scamper back to your kitchen and whip up something me and my friends can eat, or I'll make sure Randy fires you before the night's finished."

"As you wish," Becky replied demurely, lowering her eyes to keep her nemesis from seeing the sparks which surely flew out of them. Returning to her sanctuary, she pulled out a stalk of celery and smiled wickedly at her simple idea to please the vile woman.

It went against her grain to not tamper with the time-tested treat as she slathered peanut butter into the hollow of the celery. After placing raisins along the top, she chopped the stalks into bite-sized pieces and arranged them artfully onto a serving platter.

"That should be good enough," she muttered as she lifted the tray and made to exit the kitchen again.

"What do you have there?" Mabel asked, coming up behind her and peering over her shoulder.

"Ants on a log. The diva insisted we had some vegan options so I thought she'd enjoy this. She'd better, because I'm not making another thing for her."

Mabel chuckled as she shook her head. "You're playing

with fire, girl. Go on, get out there. I think I hear the car pulling up front."

Grinning at Mabel's uncanny hearing ability, she said, "I'll never understand how you can hear that over the noises in here."

"I haven't been wrong yet. Now get yourself out there so Randy'll see you right off. Make sure you offer him your assistance rather than letting Katy try to manhandle him."

Wrinkling her nose in distaste, Becky realized Katy would try to do such a predictable stunt if only to get her hands all over his body. Really, that woman knew no bounds of decency. With a pep to her step, she carried the tray out and left it at the far reaches of the dining room so Katy would have to leave the party if she wanted to get something for her delicate palate to eat.

Straightening out her blouse, she fidgeted with her hair, and brushed her palms together. Noticing the moisture forming on her palms, she absently wiped them down the sides of her dress pants. Her nerves seemed to be getting the best of her.

Stepping out into the foyer, she made straight for the front door and let herself out without anyone noticing her. Letting out a sigh of relief, she almost jumped out of her skin as Reggie chuckled right next to her where he reclined in one of the porch rockers.

"I know the feeling. I came out here for some peace and quiet. It looks as though we're going to get to have a private reunion with Randy since his car's just now pulling up." He tipped his chin to indicate the dusty car just then turning into the circular drive to park at the bottom of the stairs.

"You scared me," Becky replied, her hand clutching the

neck of her blouse as she tried to calm her racing pulse by taking several deep breaths. She turned to see James rounding the back of the car so he could open Randy's door for him. She grinned at James' jaunty step and realized all of the ranch hands had really missed Randy's presence.

The dozen or so songs which she had created in his absence did nothing for the emotions she felt in that moment. Stepping forward, she wished she had the confidence to race down the stairs and jump into his arms. Would he think she was out of bounds as his employee? Would he be just as glad to see her? If Mabel were correct, then he would twirl her around and kiss her soundly on the lips in front of everyone.

But none of this happened. She stayed rooted to the porch as the front door swung open behind her and the crowd of friends poured out until they all but obscured her sight of Randy. Their cheers echoed all around them as Katy took her place beside Randy where she placed her arm around his waist to make a great show about helping him into his house.

Becky wanted to slap the woman's hands away from her man, but she did nothing. Seeing the pleased look on Randy's face had her realizing her dreams of a future with Randy had all been inside her own mind. He was in his element. His friends surrounded him as he spoke animatedly with them.

Turning around, she made her silent escape back into the house. Not wanting to be discovered by anyone, least of all Katy, she retreated to the safety of her own bedroom where she quietly shut the door and leaned on it as tears raced down her cheeks. This day could not get any worse.

Even before the car came to a stop in front of his house, he could see both Becky and Reggie standing on the porch. It warmed his heart to have her waiting for his arrival and he could hardly wait to wrap his arms around his girl and thank her for helping him in his time of need. At first, he had been hurt by her lack of visiting while he had been bored out of his mind at the hospital, but he understood her dislike for hospitals in general.

He waited for James to come around and open his door, the anticipation of his reunion causing his heart to race. No sooner had his foot touched down on the dry soil of the driveway than the front door opened and all of his closest friends poured out of the house. His delight at seeing them all here at his house almost overwhelmed him.

When Katy appeared at his side, he cringed slightly as she slung her arm behind his back. Admittedly, he was glad for her assistance as his muscles remained weak from the ordeal in the hospital. The doctors assured him that his strength would return swiftly as long as he did not try to overextend himself too soon.

"What're you all doing here?" Randy asked, not addressing anyone in particular, yet making certain to avoid eye contact with Katy. He knew she would take it as an invitation to insinuate herself even more into his life.

"Man, we wouldn't miss your homecoming," Markson called out, clapping Randy lightly on his shoulder. "You gave us all a scare."

"You and me both," Randy joked lightheartedly. His eyes roamed the small crowd to discover where Becky had gone.

His search ended as Katy pulled him forward to get him inside. He willingly stepped forward, eager to relax in his comfy chair in the living room.

The entourage followed him into the house. Randy's eyes widened with appreciation of all of the decorations. Although, they were a bit over the top, he knew exactly who had orchestrated the whole thing. It made him feel slightly guilty that Katy would go to so much trouble, yet he was not petty enough not to say thank you.

"The house looks very festive," he managed.

"Yes, I arranged everything. Come sit down and you can tell us all about your recovery," Katy beamed.

As the evening wore on, Randy became concerned about Becky's absence. Even though he diligently searched for her, she was nowhere to be seen. With the excuse of needing to use the bathroom, Randy excused himself from the crowd so he could make his escape to the kitchen to inquire.

He opened the swinging door and only found Mabel standing at the center island, carefully preparing another tray of food for their guests. "Hey, Mabel. Thank you so much for everything. The food's been great."

Looking up and smiling at her favorite boy, she wiped her hands on her apron as she walked around the island to stand in front of Randy. "You still look pale. Give me a hug I'm not soon to forget." She held out her arms and waited for him to come closer.

Readily complying, he stepped closer and wrapped his arms tightly around his second mother. His mind wished this could have been Becky, but he still loved feeling the pats on his back from the hands of someone who knew him best. When he pulled away, his eyes showed his concern.

Being as perceptive as ever, Mabel said, "I'll tell Becky to come out of her room. She'll be in the living room shortly. You go on back to your guests while I talk with her."

"Is something wrong?" Instantly Randy wanted to forget all about his guests and go fix whatever problem Becky might have.

"Only a problem of the heart. She's a tad jealous of Katy's attention toward you."

"What? That's crazy. I didn't ask Katy to come here. Maybe I should just talk with Becky…"

"Nope, not this time. I'll take care of her."

"Fine, but if she's not out there in the next ten minutes I'll be coming right back."

"It's good to see you so feisty again." Mabel smiled, patting his arm lovingly.

Randy reluctantly turned around, hesitating only a second at the door, before pushing it open. The sound of his friends' laughter carried through the house. He missed times like this. Maybe it was a good thing to have everyone here for a while. His steps carried him forward until he found himself back in his favorite chair.

"Randy, I'm glad your back," Katy practically purred.

Instantly suspicious of her tone, Randy turned his attention to her. Usually, when she used this tone, trouble swiftly followed. "Why's that?"

"I found out something rather distressing about one of your employees."

Seeing her eyes gleaming with excitement only further put him on notice. "Who? What did you find out?"

"It's that new cook your parents hired."

All heads turned toward the doorway as Becky entered

the room. Her smile froze on her lips when the room went silent. She stopped in her tracks.

"What about Becky?" Randy pressed, ready to defend the girl who had won his heart.

Katy leaned forward, intent on drawing out the show to her advantage. "Do you know who her father is?"

"No, nor do I care."

"I think you'd better care. Her father is none other than the commissioner who's trying to push the highway through your land. Don't you think it's rather convenient that she'd come to work here? She and her father are working together to get inside information to use against you. Wake up, Randolph. You've been played like a fiddle."

Anger rose in Randy, his head turning toward Becky. The look of guilt on her face condemned her more than her words ever would. "Is this true, Becky? Is your father the commissioner?"

Becky's mouth opened but no sound came out. She shook her head. "Yes, but it's not what you think…"

"I think you should probably pack your bags. We don't have any room for spies in this house." Randy stood up and took a menacing step toward her. Never before had he felt so embarrassed, especially with all of his friends surrounding him. As soon as he saw Becky run from the room, he rounded on Katy. "Why did you wait until now to share this with me? How long have you known?"

Katy stood up, her face set in hard lines as her eyes sparkled with glee. "I only found out today. I thought you should know you have a traitor in your midst."

"I'm feeling tired. I'm going to go lie down."

"I'll help you," Katy offered, her hand reaching out to take his arm.

Pulling away angrily, he answered, "I think you've helped me quite enough."

"Randolph, don't speak to me in that tone."

"I'll speak to you however I wish in my own home."

"Are you breaking up with me?" She crossed her arms defensively.

A bark of laughter escaped from his lips at the irony of it all. "Katy, you and I have been finished since the moment you left this house the first time. Not only did you insult my parents for their choice of staff, you cared more about your own life than my grief over losing my parents. I can't believe I'd have to explain this to you."

"But I told you why I didn't come see you."

"Too little, too late. We don't share the same goals for our future. Mine's here at the ranch and yours is in the city. We were doomed for failure." He turned and walked out of the room.

By the time he reached the base of the stairs, Katy caught up to him, her hand clamping down on his arm to prevent him from walking away. With a hushed whisper, she announced, "I just had to check to make sure we were both on the same page. I've found someone else. Goodbye, Randolph. I hope you have a nice life."

Randy watched her twirl away to grab her purse from the side table. A piece of paper slid unnoticed onto the floor. She strode over to the living room and called out, "Jack, it's time for us to leave."

The man he barely noticed in the crowd before came

forward, his hand automatically dropping to the small of her back with more than a little familiarity. "Is everything okay?"

Katy glared back at Randy as she spoke to her boyfriend, "Everything's all settled. The sooner we get out of this dump, the better I'll feel."

Feeling the need to bite his tongue to keep from making a snide reply he would certainly regret, he waited until the door shut behind the pair before he went to pick up the paper. His eyes immediately recognized Becky's neat handwriting. The note crumpled in his fist as he decided to head back into the kitchen to vent with Mabel. She was always his voice of reason.

How could everything have fallen apart so fast? On his ride home, he had such great plans for his future. Now, he felt as if someone had stabbed him in the back and twisted the knife. A couple of someone's in fact, if he included Becky in the same crowd as Katy.

CHAPTER 22

The tears blurred her vision as she raced back through the kitchen and into her assigned quarters. Never before had she been so embarrassed. Randy had no right speaking to her in such a manner. He had not even let her defend herself before he judged and executed her dreams of staying at the ranch. She would never return.

With angry swipes, she slung her personal items into her suitcase. The room looked like a storm had blown through, but she hardly cared. She had to leave before Mabel could try to stop her.

With her suitcase in one hand and her guitar in the other, she left the house for the last time. Her footsteps faltered as she realized she would have to drive the car Randy had given her since she had sold her old one. Then her anger reasserted itself as she convinced herself that he at least owed her the fancy vehicle in exchange for the treatment she had received from him.

With the remote, she popped the trunk and threw her suitcase inside. She carefully placed her guitar into the back seat before she got into the driver's seat. The tears had stopped as soon as her anger overtook her emotions.

She threw the car in reverse until she cleared the other cars beside hers. Her mind raced with reckless exhilaration as she put the car into drive and pushed the gas pedal down as far as it would go. The tires kicked up a dirt into a rooster tail behind her as she fought to control the steering wheel as the car fishtailed. Backing off the gas slightly, the car straightened out and she raced down the long driveway.

Before she knew it, she spotted another car ahead of her. They appeared to be going slow to keep from getting any dirt on the fancy paint job. Seeing plenty of space to pass them, Becky shifted her car to the side of the driveway to pass them on their right-hand side. As she blasted past them, she glanced over to see Katy glaring back at her.

The car was lost behind her in a plume of dirt. An almost hysterical laugh escaped Becky's lips. Rather than stop the sound, she let it go. It felt good to laugh at how ridiculous Katy had been to her. A dirty car was nothing compared to all of the dirty words which had been slung at her.

When she reached the end of the driveway, she stopped. She did not have a plan. The apartment she had rented was now leased by someone else. That only left her father, yet she had no intention of going to him while she felt so broken. Once again, he had managed to blow up her life.

～

"WHAT'S WRONG, RANDY?" Mabel asked as she twirled around at the sound of the door cracking against the cabinet with the force of his entry into the kitchen.

"Where is she?" he snarled.

"Who? Becky?"

"Yes! We need to get some things straightened out before she leaves."

"Leaves? Randy, you're not making any sense. What happened in the last couple minutes to get you so upset? And why would you think Becky was going to leave?"

"Katy informed me of why Becky was actually here and she didn't deny it when I confronted her."

"I don't know what you're talking about but I'd imagine she's probably in her bedroom. I could go check…"

"Don't bother, I'll do it myself," he cut her off rudely before brushing past her to enter the servants' quarters. As soon as he stood in her doorway, it was evident she had left in a hurry. With a snarl of frustration, he turned on his heel and stomped back into the kitchen. "She's gone! I don't need any more proof than that!"

"Sit down and tell me from the start," Mabel directed curtly.

The tone of her voice immediately took Randy back to his childhood. She only used that tone when she was getting ready to scold him for some trouble he had caused. With his shoulders slumped, he walked over to the kitchen island where he sat down on one of the stools. "What's wrong with me, Mabel? I seem to have an uncanny way of picking the very worst women to fall for."

Mabel poured two cups of coffee and set one down in

front of him as she took the seat next to his. Taking a sip, she remained silent.

Randy knew this tactic as well. Mabel would give him the silent treatment until he apologized for his rude behavior. "I'm sorry for speaking to you that way, Mabel. You didn't deserve it."

"You're right; I didn't. Now that we've gotten that out of the way, would you mind telling me what happened?"

He threw the wadded paper onto the island so he could cup his hands around the warm mug. He stared at the black liquid as if in a trance. For the next several minutes, he shared the entire story with his best friend.

Rather than tell him what he wanted to hear, Mabel said, "Sometimes, you can be incredibly stupid. Don't you see that you've been played by Katy? She already had another boyfriend and she wanted to make sure you wouldn't find happiness without her. It's the oldest trick in the book for vindictive souls like her."

"Really? Do you think so? I mean, why would Becky leave in such a rush unless it were all true?"

"Wouldn't you leave if someone accused you in front of a group of people? You embarrassed her...no, I take that back. You mortified her." Mabel tapped her fingernails on the granite countertop. She pointed to the wad of paper and asked, "What's that?"

"A note from Becky that fell out of Katy's purse when she left," Randy answered. Even as the words fell out of his mouth, he realized how wrong it sounded. There no reason why Katy should have a note from Becky which was addressed to him.

More than a little curious, Randy picked up the paper and

began to flatten it out. After unfolding it, his eyes swiftly scanned Becky's confession written within. Feeling as small as an atom, he pushed the note over to Mabel and said, "You're right, Mabel. I am incredibly stupid."

Mabel merely read the opening lines before she declared, "You're going to have to go after her."

"I'd have no idea where to look. She could have gone anywhere."

"Jeez, Randy, would you start using the brains the good Lord gave you? Tell Hector to get the helicopter going. You'll be able to cover ground much faster than she ever could, even in that fancy car you gave her."

Randy jumped up from the stool and kissed Mabel on the cheek. "You're amazing! Do you know that?"

"Absolutely! It's about time you noticed. Use the phone in here to get Hector moving." She pointed where he should go, not trusting him to recall its location in his present state of mind.

"Right! Good thinking." He did as he was bid and then turned around to smile at Mabel. "We're going to find her and bring her back home! You should have heard how excited Hector was at the idea."

"I can imagine." Mabel stood up and said, "You can't go crawling back to her without something to give her and I've got just the thing. Cookie just brought it in." She left Randy staring after her in confusion as she went into the pantry. A few seconds later, she returned with a bouquet of beef jerky roses.

"Is that Cookie's beef jerky?" Randy's brow wrinkled with confusion. "You really think I should go to her bearing beef jerky roses?"

"Yes; I think it's perfect. After all, you're a cattle rancher and she loves Cookies' beef jerky. I'd say it's a win-win situation."

FLYING over the open countryside never seemed so desperate to Randy before. They had already checked the main highway toward Houston, only to discover the only car on the road had been that which Katy and Jack had driven away in. Feeling more frustrated at the time wasted, Randy had Hector turn around and push the helicopter to its top speed to cover the opposite direction.

He had no idea where Becky planned to go, but it was obvious she was doing her best to get lost in the desert. His thoughts were interrupted when Hector pointed out the windshield and said through the mic, "I'd bet money that's her."

Randy leaned forward, pulling out the binoculars he had brought with him and putting them up to his eyes. It took precious seconds before he could locate the vehicle in the sites of the device. When he did manage it, he exclaimed in excitement, "It's her! Hurry up, Hector."

Hector chuckled as he glanced around at their surroundings. "It's not like she's going to suddenly disappear, Randy. There's nowhere for her to go but on this road." Even so, he tipped the nose down to begin his descent toward the car, also allowing the speed to build.

They hovered about a hundred feet above the car for several seconds, pacing her before speeding ahead and dropping even lower. There was no way she could miss them.

When they saw her slowing down, Hector went a little further before setting the helicopter down in the middle of the road.

Leaving the rotors going at idle, he waved to Randy as he grabbed up the bouquet and exited through the passenger door. As soon as his boss was clear of the rotor wash, he increased the power and lifted off the road. Rather than wait around to see what happened, he sped off to return to the ranch.

Randy watched him leave, suddenly feeling nervous that this was a bad idea. He clutched the bouquet in his fist as he took the first step toward his future. Thinking about how close he came to losing her forever really drove home how much she had come to mean to him. He just had to convince her to forgive him.

Without realizing how it had happened, he found himself standing beside the driver's door of Becky's vehicle. He looked through the window to see Becky glaring back at him. "Can we talk?" he called out, hoping she could hear him.

Rolling the window down a mere crack, she replied, "I think you've made yourself quite clear, Randy."

"I didn't say anything right, Becky. I'll spend the rest of my life making up for ever making you feel less than your wonderful self."

"Ugh!" Becky groaned before she put the window back up and drove away from him.

Randy watched in dismay as she left him. His chest ached with the idea she really hated him. There he remained standing in the middle of the road, his eyes filling with tears, his chin resting on his chest.

"You really should get out of the road, Randy. Didn't your

parents teach you how dangerous it is out here?" Becky pulled on his arm.

"What? I thought you left me."

"I should've."

"I wouldn't blame you," he answered, following her to where she had pulled her car off to the side of the road. "These are for you." He held out the bouquet as a peace offering.

Becky squinted her eyes as she brought the roses up to get a better look at them. "Are these beef jerky?"

"Yes. They're Cookie's creation. Do you like them?"

"Well, they're definitely appropriate. What made you decide to find me after…everything?"

"I found your note."

"My note? What note?"

"The one that fell out of Katy's purse. She orchestrated this whole thing and I was stupid enough to fall for it. I never should have believed anything she said about you."

"I don't know what you're talking about. The only note I ever wrote to you was at the hospital on the day you were admitted."

"That must be the one. I never received it."

"Figures."

"Katy must have intercepted the nurse and read it herself. It's no wonder she concocted such an elaborate scheme to get even with me."

"Well, she didn't lie about my father. He is the commissioner trying to divide your property. I called him while I was driving and he confirmed it."

"That's not your fault, Becky. Why don't we get out of this heat and you can come back home where you belong."

"What would you do if I said no?"

Shrugging, Randy looked down the long, empty road behind them. "I guess I'd start walking. It's not like I'd have much choice. I didn't even think to bring my cell phone."

"So you were pretty sure of your success, huh?"

"Not at all! I figured I'd deserve whatever you planned for me. Although I did change into my running shoes. Just in case, you know."

Becky looked down and had to chuckle. She took a bite out of one of the roses and moaned with delight at the flavors of Cookie's famous smoked beef. "This's a wonderful idea, as corny as it is, and it tastes amazing. C'mon, get in the car. We can talk while I drive. I'm not saying I'll stay at the ranch, but I can't, in good conscience leave you to roast in the desert.

The ride home had them both speaking about their feelings and hopes for the future. Becky parked her car back in its regular parking spot. She turned to face Randy, her face suddenly serious. "I've decided to stay. I'd hate to let my father or Katy take one more thing from me that's good."

"That's the best thing I've ever heard." Randy's smile widened so far, his cheeks ached with the strain, yet he could not resist. Just hearing her agree to stay was a blessing, yet it was not quite what he needed from her. "I don't want you to work for me anymore, Becky."

He held up his hand to prevent her from interrupting him. "I'd be honored if you'd agree to marry me. I can't imagine my life without you. Thinking you'd left me forever broke my heart and I know I'd never be whole without you in my life. Please say yes."

"A hundred times yes. Randy, I'd love to marry you!"

Randy pulled her toward him until their lips almost touched. "I don't have to worry about any snakes in here. I'm going to kiss you like I wanted to a week ago. Only this time, I mean for this to be the first kiss of our lives together."

Becky nodded and pressed her lips against his. A soft moan escaped from her throat which only made Randy realize how precious she was to him. She was the other half to his soul. He finally found the final piece to his life.

He broke off the kiss and announced, "Let's go tell everyone the good news."

"I don't know. After what happened…"

"All the more reason. Besides, the guys will be thrilled to know I'll be the one to pay them each a million dollars. I plan on marrying you as soon as we can get everything arranged."

"You're crazy, but I still love you."

"I love you more!"

"Thanks."

EPILOGUE

(14 MONTHS LATER)

"I'm sorry your anniversary gift was a few weeks late," Randy repeated as he led Becky forward. He checked her blindfold one more time as he brought them to a stop in front of the door to her future. "Okay, you can open your eyes now!" he announced excitedly as he pulled off her blindfold.

Becky squinted in the sudden sunlight. She saw the door before her, but she had no idea what it meant, or what the building contained inside. She reached out and turned the knob to push the door open. Instead of stepping inside, her feet remained rooted where they stood outside.

Her eyes roamed over the small room with its walls covered in acoustic foam, including the ceiling. On the far wall, she could see a window leading to another room. "What've you done, Randy?"

"Something I should've done long time ago. Go inside and see if everything is how you need it." He pushed on the small of her back, propelling her forward.

A smile grew on her lips as she walked over to the far wall and discovered all of the top-of-the-line recording equipment. "I don't understand, Randy. What're we supposed to do with this? I don't have the faintest idea how all this works."

"Me neither. But I hired the best in the business to come and work for us. We're branching out of the ranching industry to include our new record label."

"I'm scared to ask what you named it," Becky teased, her fingers curling together with his as she leaned against him. His thoughtfulness never failed to amaze her.

"Big Ranch Records. I considered calling it Red Shoe Records, but I thought that might be pushing my luck." Randy gestured with his free hand to encompass the entire facility. "What do you think? Will you finally record all of your songs for me? You can be our first client. When those go number one, I'm sure we can bring in dozens of artists to work with."

"I love your optimism. I'll do it, but only because I love you more."

"Thanks, love."

Just then, Becky's cell phone vibrated in her pocket. She pulled it out and saw Amanda Stel's name appear on the screen. Frowning slightly, she tapped the answer button and put it on speaker. "What's up, Amanda?"

"Are you with Randy?"

"I am."

"Are you somewhere private?"

"As a matter of fact, we are."

"Good. We found Randy's parents."

"What?" Both Randy and Becky spoke at the same time.

"It's a long story, but we're flying out to your place as we speak. We'll be there in about ten minutes."

"Alright. We'll head back to the main house then," Becky replied. "See you in a few minutes." She hung up the phone and raised her eyes up to see Randy's incredulous look mirroring her own.

"How's this possible?"

"Remember how I told you about my cousin disappearing for fourteen months?"

"Yes. What's that got to do with my parents? Didn't that happen years ago?"

"It did, but I think the answer is the same. I don't want to assume anything. Let's get back to the house and we can worry about all that later. Randy, your parents are coming home!"

Randy pulled Becky to his chest and let his emotions run wild. His tears fell unchecked as he relived all of the horrors of their disappearance all over again. "I can't believe this is really happening."

Becky pulled away and began leading him outside. "This seems to be the day for surprises. First, my dad calls to tell us the highway has been rerouted to another location. Then, you give me this amazing recording studio. Now, your parents are alive and almost home. I guess my news of being pregnant is small beans by comparison."

"What? You're pregnant? When did you find out?"

"Just this morning. Are you happy?"

"Ecstatic! My life's more perfect than any man deserves. I'd pick you up and twirl you around if I didn't think it'd hurt our baby. Our baby! It even sounds perfect."

As soon as they stepped outside, they could hear the

distinct sound of an incoming helicopter. Even though they scanned the skies, they could not yet see it. The sound alone caused them to break into a jog to get back to the landing pad.

Neither one of them wanted to miss getting their first glimpse of Pop and Lucy. It still seemed too unbelievable, but they had to know Amanda would not lie to them.

Just as they reached the landing area, the helicopter came into view. Not only was it the biggest helicopter Becky had ever seen, but it was also painted a bright red color, so it stood out in stark contrast against the vivid blue of the summer sky.

The landing was perfectly executed, no doubt Riccan had employed the best pilot money could buy. Becky's hand squeezed Randy's harder as they both saw Randy's mother waving back at them from the back window.

"It's really them, Becky. My parents are alive!" Randy's voice sounded rough with emotion.

Becky glanced over at him, so thankful he could be reunited. "Yes. This has been the best day ever, don't you think?"

"Absolutely."

The sound of the engine cut off, and the rotors slowed to a stop before the passenger door opened. Riccan waved at them as he did the honors of opening the passenger door so his honored guests could finally step out onto their property.

Randy let go of Becky's hand to race forward and pull his mother into a bear hug, lifting her from the ground and twirling her around and around. He buried his face into her hair and let his tears fall freely. Finally, he set her down, keeping his arm around her torso as he pulled his father into a one-arm hug at his other side.

"I still don't understand what all the fuss is," Lucy announced into the sudden silence. "We've only been gone a week, but our crew somehow managed to get us terribly off course."

"Mom, I don't know what you went through, but the two of you have been missing for almost a year and a half. The State declared you both dead. Now we're going to have to come up with a plausible explanation to the press. I can't explain it, but at this point, I don't care just as long as I have you two with me for a very long time."

"Amanda and Riccan told us the same thing, but I didn't believe them," Pop spoke up. "What've we missed?"

Always the first to roll with the punches, Randy grinned at his Pop. He turned his parents around until they could see Becky. "I want to introduce you to my wife, Becky. We got married just over a year ago. Today, she told me we're expecting a baby."

"Eeee!" Lucy squealed before pulling away from her son to go hug Becky who had stepped nearer to the reunion. "This's the best news of all. We have so much planning, my dear. But first, you have to tell me all about the wedding. I can't believe I missed my own son's wedding."

"We took a million pictures, and we also have a video of everything. I promise you'll feel like you were there with us."

"I know you were with me in my heart," Randy inserted. He moved over to Becky's side and placed his arm over her shoulders as he pulled her in closer to his side. "Why don't we all go inside and celebrate this momentous occasion?"

"Yes, Amanda and Riccan, please say you can stay a while. We'd love to hear more about how you found these two."

Amanda nodded, her hand entwined with Riccan's. She looked up at her husband and said, "Riccan's the one you need to thank. He's the one who decided to widen his search area."

"I've had plenty of practice finding people from the air," Riccan added.

"Yes. I recall Becky telling me you work with local law enforcement to locate missing children. That's very generous of you to donate your time and aircraft for that."

"I love it. Especially when Amanda can be my spotter. It's how we met, actually."

"Well, that's the official story anyway," Amanda agreed cryptically.

The group moved toward the house when Becky let Randy go ahead of her so she could speak with her cousin and Riccan privately. She spoke in a low tone when she asked, "Where did you find them?"

Amanda glanced at Riccan before she answered, "They were in the same place I was. We can't really explain it more than just saying it's an anomaly concerning the Bermuda Triangle. It's well-documented that navigational equipment can malfunction in the area at certain times."

Shrugging to indicate there was nothing more she could add to the story, Amanda smiled brightly and added, "It seems congratulations are due to you. When will you be adding to our extended family?"

"I haven't seen a doctor, but I think our baby will come in about seven and a half months." Becky absently rubbed her stomach, her eyes turning dreamy at the idea of starting her family with the love of her life.

They entered the house to join the others. Becky paused in the doorway to the living room to enjoy the sight of her husband fully relaxed. As if he had radar for her proximity, he turned and caught her gaze with his own.

Holding out his hand, he beckoned for her to sit next to him on the couch. "I was just telling Mom and Pop that we'd start building a new house just over the ridge. We're going to make the best nursery for our child."

"And we'll have to be sure to plant a large tree so our children can have a tree swing," Becky added, her grin matching his own.

"Definitely. Although, we're already blessed beyond measure." Randy leaned over, completely ignoring the present company as he lost himself in the touch of her lips on his own.

Becky pulled away, knowing her cheeks burned brightly at the public display of affection. "I love you, Randy."

"I love you more," he replied. His eyes left hers as he turned to his parents. "Welcome home."

Want more?

Will these long-time enemies discover that charity isn't just for a cause?

Loving Texas Tea is the fun second book in the Billionaire's Venture Romance series. If you like wounded heroes, scheming villains, and Lone Star love stories, then you'll adore Amy Proebstel's sweet tale of taming the beast.

Curl up with *Loving Texas Tea* to strike it rich in love today!

And Amanda's Portal Fantasy

Trapped in an alternate dimension. Hunted by a sadist. With no magic of her own, can Amanda escape her relentless pursuer and get back to Earth?

Discover *The Keeper of Secrets* to cross to the other side today!

GET MY FREE NOVELLA NOW

To let others know how much you enjoyed this book, please leave a review at your favorite retailer.

To keep updated on upcoming books, visit www.AmyProebstel.com.

Receive a FREE exclusive novella,

Out of the Ashes

at https://geni.us/RomBM

by signing up for Amy Proebstel's newsletter.

You can also follow Amy Proebstel on Facebook at www.facebook.com/ATwistOnReality.

ABOUT THE AUTHOR

USA Today bestselling author, Amy Proebstel, writes epic dragon fantasy, magical realism fantasy, clean fated mate shifter romance, clean contemporary romance, and sweet young adult medical romance.

When she's not busy writing about young heroines and dragons saving the world, she spends her time binge-watching YouTube adventures, taking her husband and daughter flying, playing with her Pomeranian and Pomskies, or reading. If you like her books, she recommends you also check out Anne McCaffrey and Ava Richardson. They're the reason she started writing.

Subscribe to Amy's newsletter for a free book to get started on the journey today!

Feel free to email Amy at Amy@LevelsofAscension.com.

ROMANCES BEYOND TUALA, A FATED MATE SHIFTER SERIES
BILLIONAIRE'S VENTURE ROMANCE SERIES
THE CHOSEN, A MAGICAL REALISM FANTASY SERIES
DRAGON'S MAGIC: AN EPIC DRAGON FANTASY SERIES
SWEET YOUNG ADULT MEDICAL ROMANCE SERIES

facebook.com/ATwistOnReality

twitter.com/amyproebstel

instagram.com/amyproebstel

Made in the USA
Columbia, SC
01 January 2022

53131791R00129